MAYHEM

MAYHEM

MAYHEM

A Mystyx Novel

ARTIST ARTHUR

Recycling programs
for this product may
not exist in your area.

MAYHEM

ISBN-13: 978-0-373-22993-2

www.KimaniTRU.com

Printed in U.S.A.

For anyone who has ever been bullied or harassed, remember these words: Fearlessness, pride and strength are the path to overcoming your pain.

Acknowledgments

To my son Andre, for making me proud
and showing the strength of a young man growing into maturity.
I believe in you and your future, and love you lots!

To Asia and Amaya, for continuing to be the very best cheerleaders
a mother/author can have.

To Damon, for always being there.

To the readers, whose honesty and candor keep me on my toes.

To the bloggers and reviewers, for your continued support.
I'm still amazed and honored every time I see my name
or my book covers on one of your sites.

To Evette Porter, thanks so much for letting me tell the story
that's in my head. You do a splendid job, and I'm honored
to have the opportunity to work with you.

Dear Reader,

In the *Merriam-Webster's Dictionary,* which I like to browse through from time to time, the word *mayhem* is defined as "needless or willful damage or violence." When I first thought of Jake Kramer, I saw him as a boy whose life was filled with mayhem.

From the time Jake was born, he was destined to do something great. Unfortunately, that glory was overshadowed by pain and rage toward everyone he deemed responsible for his lot in life. In the end, Jake must choose between anger and love. And he must decide which one will define *his* destiny.

Jake's experience is like so many students today who are bullied at school. You constantly hear tragic stories of teenagers who endure the verbal, emotional and physical trauma of bullying. I thought it was important to touch on this subject, since it is becoming all too common. Maybe if more of us talked about it, we might be able to *do* something about it.

Writing *Mayhem* was an emotional journey that I knew I would have to tackle once I began writing the first pages of *Manifest.* I'm so glad that Jake has good friends like Krystal, Sasha, Lindsey and now Twan. He's one of my favorite Mystyx, so I'm glad to share Jake's story with you.

Dream big,

Artist

prologue

"welcome to eternal darkness," a disembodied voice said with just enough evil to make him the perfect spokesman for the Underworld.

It was his duty to bring them here. For a coin or two he became the ferryman. But in his mind he was so much more. They all underestimated him and treated him with disrespect for the lowly job he had to perform. What they didn't realize was that he came from rulers and gods more powerful than even Zeus or Hades. He was the ultimate, and in time they would soon see that.

Using his staff to guide them through the dark, murky depths of the River Styx, he transported the dead—the spirits—who sought the Underworld. After he delivered them to the gateway, they were doomed never to walk the Earth again. They were forever vanquished to the depths of Hades. But not him. No, there was another destiny for him to fulfill.

His frail body was hunched over, with a thick black robe draped around him, standing in the middle of the small boat. For those brave enough and curious enough to look over the side of the boat, their fear was mirrored in the black waters below. Thick and covered in a layer of smoke, the River Styx was a waterway plagued by evil.

After dropping off his last passenger, he headed back up the river in the opposite direction. There, just beyond the caves of the Furies, he saw an underground burrow. Pulling his boat alongside the soil, he jumped out and hurried along a trail. It would never do to be seen walking along this path—the one that passed Persephone's lair. Hades was jealous of Persephone, who targeted anyone going near her lair as fair game. He wasn't afraid of the god, but wanted to avoid attention if he could.

Slipping through the shadows, he came to the entrance of the burrow and ducked inside. It was chilly, the walls an iridescent blue surrounded by darkness. His cloak was still around his shoulders and he wrapped it tighter around his frail body. His feet moved fast, anxious to finish this last deed, once and for all.

Out of the shadows, faster than light, the beast appeared, stopping him in his tracks.

"What do you have for me, ferryman?"

He hated the beast, hated the demeaning tone the creature used with him, the inflection that was just a hair above condescension. Well, this was the last time. The power he needed was within his reach. He wanted it so badly his fingers shook as he pulled the sack of coins from his cloak.

"It is done," he said.

Yanking the pouch from his hands the creature looked at it. Dark shadowy hands opened it as saliva dripped from its sharp, protruding fangs. "It is enough," it half spoke, half growled after counting the coins. "Go and seek your reward."

He did not need to be told twice. Walking away from the beast as quickly as his feet could take him, he left the dank hovel behind him once and for all. Just as he neared the boat, the ground began to rumble, forming a crack between his legs so that he had to jump to one side to avoid being swallowed up. Just a few feet away was his boat, anchored in the river.

The river.

It bubbled and spewed steamy geysers. In certain parts, circles of fire began to burn along the surface. The indigo sky grew even darker, like a smoky pitch-black oven. The air was still and he struggled to breathe.

"You dare to disobey me!" a loud, piercing voice shouted. It was unlike any beast he'd ever heard.

"Goddess," he whispered turning to look behind him but seeing nothing. Turning in all directions he searched for her in the mortal form, but failed to see her. She was here no doubt, but where?

She was Styx, the goddess of the powerful river. She was the nymph who had fought with Zeus in the battle of the Titans and the Olympians, and was thus rewarded with supernatural powers. She was here and she was definitely angry.

"Forgive me," he said, instantly falling to his knees and bowing low.

"Not this time" was her response. "I have watched you for many moons, Charon. I have felt the slights and betrayals in your every move. This is the end. You shall be forever cursed by my hand."

"No!" Charon cringed.

Her wrath was more than feared. Even the higher gods were afraid of her. Charon had known all along that this was a consequence, but he was smarter and better than any other creature on Olympus. He knew what he was doing and why he was doing it. This was his destiny. How dare she interfere!

The river calmed and Charon thought she had changed her mind. Why, he would never know, but he chanced to look up. Above, the sky remained dark. Then two huge orbs of light appeared. One a fiery yellow, the other an iridescent white—the sun and the moon. Suddenly, the two orbs connected, one fully covering the other until all was completely dark.

Charon felt himself soaring, but to where he had no idea. What he did know was that this was not over. No matter what she did, whatever his punishment, Styx would not have the last word.

She would not destroy his destiny.

one

Fear—to be afraid or apprehensive
Merriam Webster's Dictionary

It's hot as hell out here.

I can't help but focus on the excruciating heat. Beads of sweat are forming long lines and marching down my bare back like a charging army. Late August in Lincoln usually brings heat and humidity, but this is insane.

We—me and the rest of the Mystyx—already researched what scientists are calling "the hottest summer ever." They think they're so smart, such know-it-alls, but they don't have a clue. Blame it on El Niño, a disruption of the ocean's atmosphere in the Pacific, because that's what the experts say. It's what all their computers and charts and graphs say. But it's a lie. A vicious cover-up, or maybe they just don't know the real answers. Maybe this other plane is invisible to normal human beings, and since I'm far from normal I know all about it. I guess that could be an excuse. What I know for sure is that this weather stuff is supernatural. What's going on in Lincoln and possibly all over the world has more to do with good versus evil than science.

Unfortunately my dad isn't trying to hear any of that. He's what they call an ordinary human, I guess. No powers that I know of is what I mean. I guess they skipped him like they did my grandpa. But my great-uncle, William, had them and I have them. Now if I could just figure out how to handle them, then maybe I could be of some help to the Mystyx.

In the meantime, I've got Dad's "to-do list" to deal with. He wants me to take down the back fence, the old, dilapidated piece of crap that should have been taken down long before that tornado swept through town a couple of months ago and ripped it apart. Yeah, Lincoln, Connecticut, had a tornado, and for the first time in all the years that I can remember, the residents of this small town finally recognized the weirdness that goes on around here. They couldn't believe it. The car they'd parked in front of their house ended up three or four blocks down the street. The winds even blew the roofs off some houses. There was a lot of talk around town about global warming and even the world possibly coming to an end. I wanted to tell them that it had nothing to do with global warming, but they'd never believe me. Half of them don't even acknowledge me.

But get this, just a few weeks ago New York was hit by two tornados in the same day. And before that, Maryland had an earthquake. Right in the middle of the hottest summer ever.

Nobody would ever believe it had to do with the supernatural. To be honest, about a year ago I wouldn't have believed it myself. But now I know. Scratch that, I feel the change. I'm different now, the air I breathe, the things I see, everything is different. I don't know if that's for better or worse, but we'll see.

Back to the fence or Dad'll be spittin'-nails mad at me when he gets home. The walk from one end of the yard to the other isn't far, and on any other day this chore would have just been tedious. But today it's downright miserable, with the humidity choking the life out of me. I glance up toward the sky and wonder if there's someone I can communicate with up there—tell them to turn the thermostat down a couple of notches to give me a break. Of course that doesn't work, but the brilliance of the sun burns my eyes. I keep staring though, wondering if somewhere in that big sky there's a place for me—a purpose that only I can fulfill.

Lately my thoughts have been drifting along those lines. Not that I'd tell anybody, because I'm not the philosophical type. Still, I can't help but think about all the changes I've been going through. And I'm not just talking about adolescence. That's to be expected. What I'm mostly concerned with is the freaky stuff, like my physical strength and power, and how it's growing as I get older. I gained a few pounds over the summer, not like fat, but muscle. When I step out of the shower and look into the cracked mirror on the back of the bathroom door, I can see the changes. My arms and legs look like they belong to an athlete, maybe a track star. Except I think I'm a little on the heavy side to be a runner. Still, I look like I've been working out, but I haven't. And the things I can lift are just crazy. I know I'm not supposed to do anything in public, nothing that will draw attention to me. But when Dad was changing a tire last week, the old worn-out jack started to slip and I actually had to hold the front of the car up while he slid from underneath. Had I not done that Dad would be dead. But the look Dad gave me after that incident wasn't good either. However, I've lived with that look of disapproval and confusion for a long time now. I'm used to it.

Me, Dad and Grandpa have been living together forever. My mom left when I was six and Grandma died a couple years after that. So it's just been the three of us, in this old dilapidated house with one raggedy twelve-year-old car and now, no fence. I don't know where my mom Cecelia Ann Kramer is. On good days that thought doesn't bother me. Today, it didn't until this moment.

I pick up a few two-by-four planks, actually ten. There's nobody out here to see how easily I carry the long, heavy wood and walk with ease across the yard to the big pile accumulating on the other side. It's important that nobody knows about our powers. Besides, it's a known fact that whatever people don't understand they fear, and whatever they fear they kill. Now, I'm not a huge fan of my life right now, but I'd rather keep breathing as long as I can.

Move the boards.

"I am," I respond to the voice as if my dad's behind me giving me grief about taking so long to get this project done. I don't see what the big hurry is. He just has another six or seven things on his list for me to do today. Like I'm the guy version of Cinderella, but a lot less attractive.

Wait a minute, Dad's at work. Turning around, I look to see who's there. Nobody.

Figures.

As I grow stronger, things also get weirder. As if I needed any help in that department.

Move the boards!

This time it sounds like a command. I hear it and then I feel it move throughout my body like a long, cold shiver. Instead of responding I drop every board on the ground, jumping back to keep from hitting my toes. Everything around me is still, except my biceps ripple and flex, like something's moving under my skin. I take a tentative step, and there's a pulsating sensation in my thighs that's moving down my legs to my calves.

Move them.

A little calmer this time the voice echoes in my head. I know there's nobody there, but then again there is. *He's* there, in my head, talking directly to me.

Focus on your power and move them.

The words sort of float over me now, like lines of poetry—that is, if I were a poet, I guess. Without thinking I look down at the boards. My goal is to get them stacked on the other side of the yard so the guy that lives down the block can put them on his pickup truck later this afternoon. Inhaling deeply, my eyes remain fixed on the two-by-fours until they levitate off the ground and fall neatly in a pile fifty feet away.

The sun on my back seems to burn with greater intensity, as if its rays are actually fueling my power. I know I'm not alone. I feel another presence, feel it deep inside of me.

Come to me, the voice implores.

The logical response would be *no.* My lips move to form the word, but my body has other ideas. Before I can make a decision I'm turning around, walking back to the spot where I picked up the last stack of two-by-fours. I know what's going on, at least part of it. This is about my powers. It's about the darkness that's been taunting us—this mission that Fatima, the Messenger, told us about.

It's my turn now.

My feet seem to know exactly where to go, which is good because I don't have a clue. I find myself standing in the corner where the fence forms a right angle and drop down to my knees. There's a hole in the ground, like maybe a dog got into our yard and buried its bone over here again. My hand goes right into that hole. Dirt and whatever is squirming around in my fingers. I feel something—actually, I feel a lot of something around my hand and wrist. But this is something hard, maybe important. I give it a tug, because that's all I really need to do even though my arm's in this hole up to my elbow now. But in seconds I pull it out and stare at what I've retrieved.

What I am holding, besides a bunch of dirt and a couple of worms, looks like a scroll. Tapping it against my thigh the dirt goes flying, worms slither away and I hurriedly pull the thin thread holding it together apart to unwrap it.

"Crap!" Enthusiasm about my find dies quickly as I see that whatever is printed on this scroll is in some language I can't decipher. It's certainly not in English.

In time you will know exactly what it says. It is your destiny, Jake.

"Okay, who are you and what do you want?" I ask aloud, because if I'm going to be haunted by someone or something *else* I'd like to at least know what it is.

In time. You will know everything in time.

"Yeah. Right."

The first thing you learn in this supernatural world is that people and things are never what they seem. Everything is cryptic. It's like you have to learn everything all over again. I really wish there could just be like one huge manual with all the answers, like a Wikipedia for the paranormal.

Walking toward the house I barely resist the urge to kick something or yell because of the growing impatience that seems so much a part of me now. I'm like a walking bundle of nerves lately. It's my power, I know. I've got to get a handle on it. I know that, too. But sometimes knowing something is only half the battle.

In my pocket I feel the vibration a second before my cell

phone rings. It's one of those prepaid cell phones. Dad is not about to take on another monthly bill. So only Sasha, Krystal, Pop Pop and now Lindsey have the number. At the moment, I really don't feel like talking to any of them, but I answer anyway.

"Hello." My voice sounds gruff, anxious. I know it, but it's too late to take it back.

"Hi, Jake. It's Krystal."

And just like that—the sound of her voice—melts away the anxiety.

"Oh, hi," I mumble, dropping the scroll and rubbing the dirt off my hand on my pants leg. Like she can really see my dirty hands.

"Um, are you busy?"

I don't answer right away. Don't want to seem too desperate to see her. "Ah, no. What's up?"

"I'm at the cemetery and I found something I think you should see."

"I'll be right there."

So much for not sounding desperate.

two

I could be in love with Krystal Bentley. In fact, I think I am. The million-dollar question is does she feel the same way about me? I feel like I've loved her forever when I know its really just been a few months since I met her.

Sasha talks about how different she and her boyfriend Antoine Watson are, but I swear you can't tell. Those two are so in tune with each other you'd think they were born to be together. I wonder if that's possible. If there's only one person born to be with another in the universe. If so, is Krystal the person for me?

I guess Sasha means she and Twan are different because she has lots of money and he doesn't. Or it might be because she's Latina and Twan's black. If that's the case, Krystal's black and I'm just white. I think her family is better off than mine, but not just in terms of money. My dad makes decent money, enough to take care of us and all Pop Pop's medical bills. We just don't have a lot of extras. Their house is bigger and her stepdad's a big shot at the company where he works. But the biggest difference between us and the one that I think of most is that Krystal has her mom. As much as they've had their ups and downs since moving here, her mom has always been there for her. And now they're spending all this time together in church. Okay, that probably sounds like I'm against church but it's really not like that. What bothers me is that Krystal has a mom to spend time with. And I don't.

I think the consensus is that boys need their fathers, and I don't doubt that. I'm glad my dad's in my life. But there's always been something missing, like a part of me walked out the door when my mom did. I don't know if she meant it to be that way, but it was. I give the impression that my life's been okay without her—me and Dad do. But it's a lie. Our lives, where she's concerned, are a lie.

For years I blamed myself, wondering what I could have possibly done to chase my mother away. Maybe I didn't clean my room enough. She was always after me about making up my bed and putting my shoes in the closet. I was just a messy kid, so I ignored her. And I never ate broccoli. The more she cooked it, the more I shoved it under my shirtsleeve and dumped it out afterward. I hated how it looked and smelled and wanted to barf at the idea of putting it in my mouth, let alone chewing and swallowing it. Could that have finally pushed her over the edge?

I'm older now, so I think her leaving because her kid wouldn't eat broccoli is about as likely as Christmas coming in July. Still, there's some guilt there—deep inside of me. I don't know what I could ever do to get rid of it. She's gone and that's that. I need to get over it.

Just like I need to figure out what I'm going to do about Krystal. Am I finally going to make a move or just keep harboring this secret crush like a coward?

"Hi," she says, looking up from the spot where she's squatting, surrounded by tombstones.

I know this sounds creepy considering the circumstances,

but every time I see Krystal Bentley she gets prettier. At first I thought I was just being dramatic, sounding like some dude in a chick flick, but it's really true. It started when she first came to Settleman's High and I saw her get off the bus. We became friends and I began hearing her voice all the time. That only added to what I liked about her. Now, this summer, since we're connected by the Mystyx stuff, I see her at least a couple times a week. I actually look forward to it.

Her hair looks soft. But I never touch it, because, well, I don't know. I just don't.

"Hi." Finally, words—or should I say *a* word—tumbles out of my mouth. I swear she must think I'm the biggest loser ever. "What's up?"

There, now I've said three words. Let the celebration begin.

"I want you to see what I found," she says, and stands up slowly.

Krystal's about three or four inches shorter than me. She has on shorts that seem really short. Or maybe her legs are just really long. God, could I be a bigger geek?

"What'd you find?" Clearing my throat so it doesn't crack and I end up sounding like one of the Chipmunks. I shift from one foot to the other. Maybe she won't notice how nervous I get around her. Well, why wouldn't she? After all, I'm stumbling over words and dancing around like I've gotta pee. Please, get a grip.

All right, take a deep breath and stop it. Silently admonishing myself usually helps me get my act together. I mean, since my dad isn't around a lot, I usually don't have anyone telling me what to do. So I sort of just tell myself what to do. And that little tidbit I'll keep to myself.

Now, okay, she's a girl and I'm a boy. It's cool. Everything's cool.

"It's a grave," she says.

Well, I guess I could have figured that out, since we're in a cemetery. "Whose grave?"

She doesn't answer, just steps to the side so I can see for myself.

William Beaumont Kramer

Beloved Son

August 1933—

"My great-uncle's grave."

"I had this feeling, like right here in the pit of my stomach," she says, wrapping an arm around her midsection.

She's wearing a charm bracelet, silver with a couple of charms hanging from it. I wonder what they are. Again, wanting to touch her.

"Nobody's there, but somebody is. They want something. I'm getting kind of used to it now, their calling."

"The ghosts?"

"The spirits. I like to think of them as wayward spirits now. Ghost sounds scary and I'm not afraid anymore—not of them anyway. So, it started out like a nagging feeling when I woke up this morning. I ran some errands with my mom, you know she's helping out with that church bazaar."

I nod because I remember her telling us about this a few weeks ago. Krystal's mom is really active in the local church now. I think it's Baptist but I'm not sure because we never go. Still, I think it's helping Krystal and her mom get closer and it's probably what helps Krystal deal with the ghosts—or rather, spirits. I don't know how exactly, but it seems to make sense.

"Anyway, the whole time I'm at church the feeling gets stronger, more persistent. I went and just sat in a corner, thinking about the feeling, opening myself up to whatever was trying to get in contact with me."

Krystal sounds like a real medium now—whatever that is. I've never heard a medium talk before. But what I mean is that she sounds like she knows what she's doing, how to handle her power and all that.

"I kept waiting for a voice or an image to appear but there was nothing. Just this sensation and this urge to go someplace. The urge led me here. When I looked down at the stone and saw the name, I called you."

"Because he was my great-uncle."

"But I thought your grandfather said he just disappeared. Not that he died."

I shrug because I don't know the right thing to say. "I guess he would have died sooner or later."

"But did he die here in Lincoln? Is his body really buried here?" She looks back down at the tombstone. "There's no date of death."

I nod. She's right. That was the first thing I noticed after seeing the gravestone. "And he's not here? I mean, he hasn't said anything to you and you haven't seen him, or his gh... spirit?"

"No."

"Odd."

"Nothing new there," she says with a chuckle.

Did I mention I love to hear her laugh?

She didn't do that a lot when we first met. But now, as time has gone on, she's relaxed and she laughs more.

It's still hot out here. The sun's blazing down on us even

though there are large shade trees in the cemetery. But she looks cool and pretty, not drenched in sweat like me.

"I guess I can ask Pop Pop if he remembers anything else about his brother or if his parents said anything about burying him here. I don't see why they would go through all the trouble of marking a grave if he isn't really here."

"Something's here," she says quietly. "I can feel it. I just don't know what or who. All I know is it's a warning. It's in the air, all around this area. It's like a warning that's meant for us."

"Of course it's meant for us. Any and everything freaky in this town is meant for us," I say as I walk away from Krystal toward the headstone next to my uncle's. It reads James Balderson. I wonder who he was or how he died.

"It's creepy here." I don't know what else to say. I don't have answers but I feel like Krystal and I should be talking about something. I mean, we're here in the cemetery and there's nobody else. Unless you count the dead and they're not gonna talk to me. "Looking at each headstone makes me wonder about each person, who they were before they died."

"I come here a lot."

I turn. She's walking right behind me. "You do?"

She shrugs. "I don't think I really have a choice. Sometimes it's peaceful, other times it's a madhouse."

She smiles like she wasn't quite sure if I was going to get the humor or not. I smile back.

"So what were you doing when I called?"

"Just stuff."

"You want to go and do something else now?" she asks.

I trip and stumble, trying to catch myself before I end up eating dirt and looking like more of a dork than I already do.

She grabs my arm, which makes me feel about two feet tall. Steadying myself, I pull away from her.

"Sorry," she mumbles.

"No." I sigh. Idiot. Idiot. Idiot. "It's not you."

We walk a little more until I realize we're leaving the cemetery. It makes sense, I don't like graveyards. And while Krystal might feel some connection here, I just feel…weird.

"You hungry?" I ask once we get to the front gates.

"Sure."

"Maggie's is just down the block."

She nods and starts to walk that way. I walk beside her, on the side of the sidewalk near the curb because that's what Pop Pop says men should do.

Maggie's is Lincoln's hippest carry-out. On Main Street across from the library there's Jeb's Diner, but that has an old-time feel with a menu full of meat loaf, pot roast, mashed potatoes and vegetables. Maggie's serves pizza, subs, fries. They also have this bar full of miscellaneous stuff like eggrolls and bean pies.

"So if your uncle's not buried there, I wonder who is?" Krystal asks as we walk.

"I wonder why they would even put the headstone there if his body is someplace else."

"Do you think he tried to run away from his powers?"

"I don't know how he could. Wherever he went, the powers went with him."

"Which means if he left Lincoln and maybe married and had kids, then they would have powers, too."

I shake my head. "No. I don't think so. The power is from the storms. Remember, Fatima said Styx controls the moon and the sun. That's how we got our supernatural powers."

"And we're supposed to use them to fight the Darkness."

"Right."

By this time we're at Maggie's. We walk down the street, talking and not really paying attention to much else. Not that there's anything else going on in Lincoln anyway. There are a couple of other shops on the other side of the street—a place that sells tacky costume jewelry, an antique store and Jerry Madison's mom's crafts store.

Coming to the light we wait, then cross the street. I get to the door first and open it for her. Pop Pop would be proud of me. He'd say, "See, Jakey boy…" Yes, he still calls me that even though I'm almost sixteen years old. He'd say, "See, Jakey boy, chivalry ain't dead, no matter what you young people think."

So I'm being chivalrous with Krystal. I wonder if she notices or if it's even something she appreciates. I really wonder if this is how Franklin treated her. Franklin's gone now, I know that. And she knows that. But still, he was her boyfriend first. That still makes me angry.

Krystal heads to a booth near the back. It's like she's reading my mind. Not that I don't want to be seen with her, that's definitely not the case. It's just that a lot of kids hang out here, especially on hot summer afternoons. Either they're at the pool or in here eating and playing video games. I don't want to be bothered with any other kids. I just want to have a slice of pizza with Krystal.

So once we sit down she looks at me like she's been waiting forever for me to sit across from her. "What?" I ask before I can think of whether it's right or wrong.

"Why do you do that?"

"What?" I say again and feel like a parakeet.

"Whenever you're around a lot of people you look down or away, and you hunch down like you don't want anybody to see you."

She's smart. "I don't."

"Why?"

I look at her for a minute, this time thinking about what I want to say first. There's so much I want to say, so much that I think about all the time, but I don't know if she really wants to hear it. Of course she doesn't, nobody does. I already know the answer.

"I don't know why I do it. Just a habit, I guess. No big deal."

She's drumming her fingers on the table. She does that a lot. It pisses Sasha off, but I usually ignore it.

"What do you want to eat?" she asks and sort of smiles a little.

"Do you miss him?" I blurt out and want to bite my tongue off the minute I do.

She blinks, looks at me, then looks away. She picks up the menu and looks at it. "Do I miss whom?"

No going back now. "Franklin."

Her eyes stay glued to the menu even though I know she already knows what's on it and what she's going to order—pizza.

She finally shrugs. "I don't know."

I think she does, but it's probably best not to continue this conversation. I mean, it's not really cool to talk about the ex when you're on a date. But this isn't really a date. We're just hanging out. I want to go on a date with Krystal—have for a very long time. But just like a lot of other things I want, it'll probably never happen.

We order and minutes later, the pizza comes, extra cheese

and pepperoni, just the way Krystal likes it. She takes a slice and the cheese oozes all over the place, steam floats from the topping as she guides it to her mouth. For a minute I think maybe she'll put the slice on her plate. But then she puts it right up to her mouth and takes a bite. As she chews, Krystal fans her mouth and I laugh.

"You do that every time," I tell her. And she does.

"I know," she says, still chewing, sucking air into her mouth to cool it off. "Can't...help...it."

So we're eating our pizza, enjoying each other's company, or at least I'm enjoying her company. Then the door opens and in walks trouble. I feel it before I even see them. And it only takes about two-point-four seconds for them to notice me and close in.

"Well, well, well. What do we have here?" says Mateo Hunter, with his close-cropped black hair and beady eyes.

His sidekick, Pace Livingston, is right beside him, dark blond hair and eerie light gray eyes. He smiles down at Krystal.

"If you were looking for a date, you could have just called me, baby," Pace says to Krystal, wrapping his hand around the end of her ponytail.

She yanks away and I instantly sit straight up in my seat, ready for anything.

"Leave us alone," I say in a voice that lacks a whole lot of conviction or confidence for that matter. But that's usually the case where these guys are concerned. It's not that I'm afraid of them, I'm not. I just don't want any trouble, or at least that's the way I used to think about dealing with them. It was just easier to fly below everybody's radar if I could. I tried to mind my own business, stay out of trouble, do my schoolwork and help my dad and Pop Pop. Lately, however, I've been thinking about my life a little differently.

"Shut up, tracker!" Mateo snaps, then reaches over and helps himself to a slice of our pizza.

"Let's go, Jake," Krystal says. She's looking at me with this concerned look in her eyes. I wonder if she knows what I'm feeling, what I'm thinking right now.

I hope not.

Strike him, the voice inside my head warns.

"Not yet, sweetheart. We're just getting to know one another," Pace says, trying to slide into the booth next to Krystal. She doesn't move over so he's kind of hanging half on and half off the seat.

Under the table my fists tighten. "Get away from her," I say through clenched teeth. Only it doesn't sound like my voice. It sounds stronger, more forceful.

Pace looks over at me like he's just realized I'm sitting there. "Make me," he taunts.

"Yeah, tracker," Mateo adds, tossing his half-eaten slice of pizza down so it falls on the table right in front of me. Bits and pieces of cheese and sauce splash onto my shirt.

"Jake," Krystal says. "Let's just go."

She reaches across the table to try and grab my arm but I pull back and push out of the booth. "I said, get away from her," I repeat to Pace.

My eyes are focused on him now. Heat is coursing through my veins like I've been injected with liquid fire. It pumps through me, making the muscles in my arms ache and my thighs tingle with what feels like more strength.

"And what if he doesn't?" Mateo asks, getting up in my face. He's so close I can smell whatever type of gel or gook he puts in his hair to make it shine like rain. He's glaring at me, hatred seething from his pores.

I know the feeling, it matches my own. He wants to fight. I want to oblige him. Every muscle in my body flexes.

"What are you going to do, tracker?"

Mateo and I are about the same height, five feet seven or so. I remember him from the Little League baseball team, the one I only played on for a half season because Dad got tired of picking me up out of the dirt—where Mateo and his friends would always push me. But that was then. I'm not seven years old anymore, and Mateo is not going to continue pushing me around.

"You don't want this," I say very slowly.

"Jake." I can hear Krystal calling my name. She's standing now. She stands by my side and grabs one of my arms. Her touch is like electricity, sizzling through my body. I want to pull away to stop the force of the connection but I can't.

"Don't, Jake," she says, her voice a little lower. "It's not worth it."

"You gonna listen to your little girlfriend, Jakey?" Pace says, stepping up behind Mateo.

"Hey, what's going on over there?" The deep voice of the manager interrupts our argument.

But it doesn't drown out everything or everyone.

Strike him. Hard.

It's the same voice from earlier, the one that feels eerily like another part of me. My fists clench and I feel my right arm lifting.

"No!" Krystal yells putting herself between me and Mateo. "Don't. Do. This."

Her eyes are serious, locked on mine as she speaks. I focus

on them, on their almond shape and root beer–brown color. Her skin looks so smooth, like Pop Pop's coffee with lots and lots of cream. Her lips are small, kind of heart-shaped, and her hair is so dark, so silky and long. My fingers are unclenching, flexing, as the urge to run them through her hair replaces the hot rage seething inside me a few seconds ago.

"Let's just leave," she says again, and this time threads her fingers through mine.

Her touch is no longer electric but warm, soothing, like it's pushing everything bad away.

"Awww, isn't that sweet," Pace taunts.

"Get out of here, all of you." The manager is right up on us now, grabbing Pace and Mateo by their shirt collars and pulling them toward the door. "You two," he shouts back at me and Krystal. "Pay your bill and get going."

With Mateo and Pace gone, my heartbeat returns to normal. Everything seems to return to normal, my muscles don't tingle and I'm no longer seething with rage. Everything except I'm touching Krystal. Or rather she's touching me. Anyway, I like it.

We walk to the counter, she's still holding my hand. I use the other hand to reach into my back pocket and pull out a ten to pay for our pizza and drinks. I'm so into the feel of her hand in mine and the way she's looking at me that I forget my change and just walk right out with her by my side.

I could stay like this forever, with her hand in mine. But the stickiness of the heat outside greets us. And on top of the streetlight on the corner we walk by there's a black bird. It looks like a crow or a raven—whatever, they're from the same family. But its beady little eyes are on me, directly on me.

Next time.

The voice echoes in my head and I look back at the bird, which opens its beak like it's the one speaking.

three

"where are we going?"

Charon was tired of hearing the question. Beside them Lor, in his dark earthly form, groaned. It was no secret that Lor didn't agree with Charon's plan to include mortals. But Charon felt differently. They'd used other mortals, possessed them and made them do their bidding, but this one was different.

"Where we will be safe, for now," was Charon's only reply.

It was hard to find a safe place here on this Earth, since there were now so many magicals. They could no longer remain in the Majestic. News of his betrayal and Styx's vengeance was spreading. The magicals were taking sides, forming allegiances, building alliances—some to him but most not. There were some who were trying to help them, the children of Styx—the Mystyx, as Lor discovered they were called. Styx wanted him to suffer, to never surface again. But Charon had other ideas. Her children had to join forces to kill him. That meant they had to band together to use their powers at the right place and the right time. Discovering their true purpose here on Earth wasn't going to be easy.

There were four of them and they were all different. Styx was smart, she had chosen wisely. Just as she had thought to protect them in some way. Charon had yet to figure out how.

That's why he'd summoned Lor. The dark beast was so hideous he couldn't reveal himself in the Majestic. He appeared as thick black smoke. This allowed him to see and hear things that others couldn't, so he could at times go undetected. It also allowed him to plant the seeds of fear in the children of Styx.

His goal was to divide and conquer. One of the Mystyx in particular was going to make that a lot easier. The boy called Jake was an open portal for darkness, his strength the perfect power to utilize. If he could simply woo him away from the others.

"Why can't we stay in Lincoln?"

Lor switched sides, covering the boy with his darkness. The boy—whose given name was Franklin but was called boy anyway—did not seem bothered by it.

There was something about this boy, something just a little dark and a bit more dangerous than the Mystyx or any of the others they'd channeled. *It wasn't obvious, in fact,* he thought. It was probably overlooked. This boy seemed inconsequential, but that was not so. Charon was positive of that fact. That's why he took him. This mortal would come in handy in his fight for power if Jake did not make the right choice.

"I can't wait until school starts. We're going to be juniors and you know what that means," Lindsey said in her usual overly excited voice.

I didn't like her when she first came to Lincoln and some days she still rubs me the wrong way. But overall I guess she's cool. Especially since we know she's a Mystyx.

But she still talks too much.

It's been a couple days since the incident at Maggie's. School is about a week away and my dad's finally letting up on all the chores. I swear I feel like I'm being abused as child labor sometimes. But today we're at the pool, just hanging out. It's a public pool, behind city hall. Some of the Richies have pools in their backyards, so this is for those who can't afford that luxury.

We got here early to grab the best lounge chairs, ones that aren't beat up and cracked. We dragged them along the deck on the opposite side of the pool from the diving board. All four of us sit and watch while Lindsey talks.

"What do you think it'll be like? Our junior year, I mean," she says to no one in particular. But we all know she expects an answer.

Krystal, who is sitting in the chair beside me with the hottest baby-blue two-piece bathing suit I've ever seen, answers first.

"Probably the same as last year. I really don't believe in that upperclassmen status thing. We'll just be regular students, enduring another year of bad cafeteria food and mediocre classes."

Sasha smiles, turning her head so that she looks at Krystal as her large-frame sunglasses slip down a little on her pert nose. "You've got a point there," she says.

"What about you, Jake? What do you think it'll be like?"

I shrug. "Just another year." What I don't say is that it's another year that I'm closer to getting out of Lincoln. I can't wait to blow this town and get on with the rest of my life. What that entails I don't know for sure. At one point I thought I'd go to college, maybe become a gym teacher or something like that. But now, with all the changes, I don't really know. What

I know for sure is that whatever adult life involves, I won't be doing it here in this town.

"Well, I think it's going to be fantastic," Lindsey says. "C'mon, let's go for a swim."

She stands first, taking off her white rhinestone-encrusted sunglasses and tossing them on her chair. Lindsey's a cute girl, I guess, if you go for that type. Petite and pert is what I call her. She's about five feet two or three and doesn't have curves, but you can definitely tell she's a girl. Her one-piece black bathing suit is simple and understated, but fits her bubbly personality for some reason.

Lindsey wears black to block out others' thoughts because she's telepathic. She says it helps her stay sane. I guess it would be kind of weird to walk around hearing everybody's thoughts all the time. I know I'd go crazy if I had to deal with thoughts other than my own.

And other than that voice that keeps popping up. The one I hear on a daily basis but refuse to tell anyone about. The one that makes me feel all-powerful.

"Yeah," Sasha adds, standing in her bright yellow two-piece. "It's hot, we need to cool off."

Sasha's the girliest of our bunch. Her long dark curly hair fans out down her back. She's real tan, too, so she looks exotic or something.

Just over her shoulder I see Antoine Watson walking toward us. Twan dating Sasha was a little weird at first, but is kind of cool now. I don't really like being the only guy in the bunch all the time. So sometimes when we hang out, Sasha brings Twan along. A good testosterone balance, I think.

And the dude is so totally hot for Sasha it's amazing she doesn't melt.

"What's up, Jake?" Twan says as he approaches, giving me a nod of his head.

I nod back. "Hey, Twan," I say because I call him what the rest of his friends call him, not what Sasha calls him.

Sasha is instantly all smiles. I turn and look down at Krystal who hasn't gotten up from her chair yet.

"You coming?" I ask and reach my hand out to help her up.

She smiles, takes my hand and stands. "Sure."

There are a lot of girls here at the pool. Some in plain old bathing suits and some in scraps of material that should be illegal, but I don't really care about any of them. The one person I really like is walking next to me.

She lets go of my hand, so I have to be content to just walk beside her. I'd love to put my arm around her like Twan's doing with Sasha, but I don't know if she wants me to. She doesn't talk about Franklin much but I know she still thinks about him. Maybe she's not ready to move on. Maybe she doesn't want to move on with me. Maybe…

"Stop daydreaming and get in," Krystal says nudging me with her elbow before slipping into the water.

I look up and notice that everybody's already in. So I jump in, pressing my knees to my chest with my arms so that I make a big splash. As expected, the girls squeal and Twan laughs, giving me a high-five once I'm in the water.

Swimming, getting closer to Krystal—it all seemed normal, fun even. But as the afternoon wore on, I felt like this was only the beginning. Not of the fun, but of the changes to come. Changes that I can't tell whether they are good or bad. Changes that make me feel weird, and somewhat afraid.

★ ★ ★

That night at the dinner table, I decide to ask Pop Pop about his brother and the gravesite.

"I saw Uncle William's grave at the cemetery the other day," I mention casually, while forking a roasted potato into my mouth. I chew fast even though it tastes fine.

Pop Pop is just poking at his food, but Dad freezes totally. I look over at him and he's giving me the strangest look I've ever seen from him.

"What were you doing at the cemetery?" he asks.

Something to know about my dad, he's not into the super-natural stuff—at all. Nope, Harry Kramer is a straight-and-narrow maintenance worker at the local utility company. He does his job and he takes care of his family. That's it. Or at least that's the way it's been since my mom left.

"Just hanging out with a friend," I say as nonchalantly as I can.

"Are you and this friend weirdos or something? Who hangs out at a cemetery?" he asks.

Dad's a big guy, broad shoulders, beefy calloused hands from using them all day at work and again at home. I've got his chocolate-brown hair as my mom used to call it, and his eyes. He wears plaid shirts all the time. I mean, every day of the week, every day of his life. I don't think I've ever seen him in anything other than a plaid shirt. It's almost like maybe he missed his calling and was supposed to be a lumberjack in-stead of a maintenance man.

I shrug. "No. Just looking for something to do around here."

"Well, why don't you try studying?" Dad says, picking up

his chicken leg and taking a huge bite out of it. He's angry, but I don't know why.

"School's out, Dad."

"You can still study. There's always something to learn, Jake. And if you want to make something of yourself you've got to have book smarts. Don't be like me, only using your hands all the time. You've got a good brain. Learn how to use that."

"He's got the power, too," Pop Pop says quietly. "No use in trying to ignore it, Harry. He's got it just like William had it."

"Not at my table," Dad says slowly. "Not in my house."

"Can't hate it away, son. It's there. Plain as day, it's there."

"Where's Uncle William?" I ask, figuring this conversation is going to happen no matter what. And Dad's going to be pissed no matter what.

"He ain't there," Pop Pop says. "Never was. My mother just wanted the questions to stop."

"Pop," Dad says like he's warning his father not to go any further.

But Pop Pop just waves his wrinkled hand at him. He drops his fork, giving up trying to mash the potatoes with it. I reach over and mash them for him. But Pop Pop just keeps looking at me.

"Be careful, Jakey. Will didn't know how to handle his power. But you, you can do it. I know you can."

"How do you know?"

"That's enough!" Dad yells, throwing his napkin onto his plate and standing up. "We will not talk about any of that hocus-pocus crap in my house."

Pop Pop frowned. "It'll be here whether we talk about it or not, Harry. It just is."

Dad shakes his head, his expression serious. "No. I won't allow it."

"Just like you didn't allow Cecilia to do what she needed to do. You see where that got you."

The look Dad is giving his father is anything but nice. I think if Pop Pop wasn't so old and frail and Dad hadn't been raised to love and respect him, my father may have been tempted to hit the old man. My father's fists are clenched at his sides and his eyes are dark. The lobes of his ears are red, which means he's about to blow.

"I don't want to hear her name in this house. You hear me? And you keep feeding my boy with this magic hoodoo and you'll be watching *Jeopardy* in that old folk's home in New Haven."

Dad storms away from the table, yelling behind him. "Eat your dinner and clean the kitchen, Jake!"

Sure. Eat my dinner. Clean the kitchen. Go to school. Get good grades. Don't ask questions.

That's what he wants from me. Always has.

Unfortunately, I have lots of questions. Always did. One of them is why did my mother leave. But I'd always known to never ask my dad that. Now I'm wondering if Pop Pop knows. For an old guy, he seems to know an awful lot about everything.

"Poor boy, never did get over her leaving," Pop Pop says when we're alone. Then he takes a deep breath and lets it out through his thin lips.

"Jake, this power is bigger than me or your dad, or even your mother. You've got an important job to do. I've been sticking around all this time just to tell you that. To guide you, I guess. Otherwise my old body would have keeled over by now."

"Don't say that, Pop Pop." I don't like to think of him dying. Even though his Alzheimer's is advancing, he also has a bad heart so he's sick a lot. But he's the only one I can talk to. I don't know what I'd do if something happened to him.

"It's okay, Jakey. I'm fine with dying—when it's my time. I still have some work to do with you, though. Some things to tell you."

"Things about the power, about the Darkness?"

Pop Pop's blue eyes look glossy for a moment. "It's more than just darkness. It's a living, breathing evil and it's coming after you and the others because it knows you're the only ones who can stop it."

"But how? How do we stop it, Pop Pop?"

"You have to choose good over evil. No matter what, Jakey. You have to choose good. Evil makes him stronger."

"And that's what he wants? To grow stronger? What happens if he grows stronger?"

"Mayhem," Pop Pop says, then coughs.

I get up and pat him on his back lightly. He coughs some more until it sounds like mucus is coming up through his chest. I reach for his glass of water and hold it to his lips. He takes a sip, then another. "All hell's gonna break loose if it gets stronger. And I mean that, Jakey. Things we've never seen here on Earth will take over. There won't be a world as we know it anymore. Evil will take over and we'll be done for."

I stand very still listening to his words and must have looked a little stunned, too, because Pop Pop puts one of his hands over mine. I look down at the spidery blue veins threading through his hand, at his long fingers and nubby nails. I don't know what else to say.

"You can beat it. Will couldn't. But you can."

"Where's Uncle William?" I whisper.

Pop Pop sighs. "Long gone. Lost to the evil years ago."

We're both quiet after that.

"But you'll do better, Jakey. You'll do better than Will did. I know you will."

That night as I lie in my bed staring out the window, through the blinds into the dark sky, I wonder how Pop Pop can be so sure when I'm not.

four

It's the first day of school.

I guess I should be excited about embarking on my junior year in high school. One more year until graduation, then off to college. Yeah, that sounds a lot better than I feel. What I really think about the first day of school is that it sucks.

I stand waiting for the bus on the same corner that I've stood on for two years in a row. With the same couple of kids I've stood beside before. Mostly it's the Goth kids that live down here by the tracks with me. The others in my neighborhood have either already graduated from Settleman's or dropped out. Probably from boredom, but at any rate they're no longer riding the ole yellow bus with me.

The bus pulls up just as I'm thinking about it. I get on, head straight to the back and take a seat by the window. Nobody will sit by me, they never do. I pull my hoodie up over my head anyway and start to stare out the window. For the next twenty minutes the bus makes the same stops it always has, picks up the same kids.

But they look different. New clothes, of course, and some have a new look. Like girls think dying and cutting their hair, wearing more makeup than last year or even shorter skirts is going to make a difference. It doesn't. They're all still stuck in this town looking at the same people day after day.

I wonder how Uncle William got out.

I mean, it's not like I can't just buy a bus ticket and head out of town. I can. I have six hundred and eighty-seven dollars saved in the pickle jar under my bed. I could go somewhere and do something else. But where and what?

I guess Uncle William had a plan. He knew where he wanted to go and he just went. Or did someone take him? That's what Pop Pop said, that Uncle William couldn't handle his power and they got him. They who?

The thing about talking to Pop Pop is that you never know when the little switch in his head that keeps him talking like a real person or reverting to his demented ramblings will kick in. I don't know how many times I've been in the middle of a conversation with him when he starts talking about things like aliens or a marble he lost when he was seven. So I usually try to get as much coherent information out of him as I possibly can.

Now I know that Uncle William is not in the grave and that he couldn't handle his powers. Did the Darkness take him? And where?

Fatima, whom Sasha contacted a couple months back, had introduced us to a new place. Or I guess I should say a new plane, a dimension between Earth and the heavens, she said. Sasha, with her powers, can travel there. But the other Mystyx, myself included, can only hear about it. That sounds crappy and feels that way, too.

Anyway, this other dimension is called the Majestic. It's the home of magical beings. So I guess it stands to reason Fatima would come from there. She says she's a Messenger. Her job is to guide us, the Mystyx, through this journey we have to take. To tell the truth, I don't have a lot of faith in Fatima and what she says. Mainly because she mostly doesn't say anything.

She speaks in this voice that's like singing all the time and she never really answers a question. It's like she waits for us to figure stuff out, dropping silly clues that just piss me off more.

Do I believe in the Majestic?

Yes. I do. There has to be a place where all this weirdness is considered normal. If we're powerful and we're on Earth, I can't help but believe there are others. We're fighting something, that's for sure. What it is and how bad it is, we only know from Fatima's warnings. And Pop Pop's. He thinks the Darkness is bad, too.

Me, I'm starting to wonder.

"Hey, you. Daydreaming again?"

I smelled her before I actually saw her. I mean, her perfume. It's soft like clouds and baby powder. And it's all around her, in her jacket, her clothes, her hair. It just hovers.

"Oh, hi," I say, swallowing hard when I finally do manage to look at her.

She takes the seat right next to me. Krystal Bentley, the girl who occupies a permanent place in my dreams.

"They switched the bus routes, so I'm on the same one with you this year," she says putting her book bag between her legs.

Her hair's in a ponytail but it's pulled around so that it drapes over her shoulder. She's adjusting her purse and stuff and I keep staring at her. From her earrings—dangling silver stars—to her clingy white T-shirt and shiny lime-green vest, she's perfect.

"What? I didn't even notice the bus route had changed." Which I didn't. It looked the same to me. Well, when I had been looking and not, like she said, daydreaming.

★ ★ ★

My last period was gym, a class that was usually easy for me. But that was before Pace and Mateo joined the class. They were seniors, but because they had some holes in their schedule, of course they opted to take the easiest course ever to pass the rest of their time in high school. And of course make the last hour of my school day hell.

Hell is probably an overstatement, but it's certainly more uncomfortable now that they're in my gym period. Lining up, the gruesome twosome are right across from me. I wish there were pockets in these gym shorts or even a hood on this T-shirt. As it is, I feel exposed, like everybody can see me, see through me. That's not good.

Today is basketball. Why does it seem like Mr. Strickman always falls back on basketball when he doesn't really have anything planned? I had him in ninth grade and he used to do the same thing. But jeez, it's the first day of school, how could he not plan something for the class that day? Maybe basketball is his plan. I chuckle because that's so lame.

Ryan Johnson is a team leader and, wonder of all wonders, star point guard of the school's basketball team. So is Pace. And since Pace is Mateo's friend, that's who his first choice is. Back and forth the choosing goes, a sort of popularity contest for boys. A ridiculous ritual that only segregates the students more, not that the teachers pay any attention to that fact. Just when I think I'm going to be the last one reluctantly selected to be on Ryan's team, Pace says my name, followed by a chuckle that's quickly echoed by Mateo and a couple of the other guys on their team.

I *so* don't want to go over there with them, but what choice do I have? I know they have something planned, I can see the look in their eyes. But I walk over there anyway, my old beat-up sneakers squeaking across the newly polished wood floors.

Thinking maybe I'm overreacting, I try to calm myself down and focus on playing the game until the bell rings. Shouldn't be too hard, right?

Mr. Strickman blows the whistle, then sits on the bleachers waiting for us to take it from there. I'm on the floor guarding Ryan in what seems like a normal play. But as soon as my team gets the ball and we start to run down court I get this bad feeling. It starts in the pit of my stomach and churns for a minute like I ate something bad. I keep moving, hoping to not look like a pansy in front of the rest of the guys.

"Heads up!" I hear about a millisecond before the ball comes barreling in my direction.

There's nowhere to go and no time to get there.

SMACK!

It actually feels more like a slap in the face as the orange ball painfully makes contact with my nose. I instantly see red.

Beyond the pain there's a quiet hush that falls over the gymnasium. Pace threw the ball. Now he and Mateo are laughing hysterically.

There's a loud ringing in my ears, vibrating throughout my body. The bottom half of my face feels warm, I figure from the blood gushing out of my nose. My eyes fix on them and something inside me is unleashed.

Next thing I know I'm walking toward them. Pace, true coward that he is, takes a step back. Mateo kind of pumps up like he's ready for whatever I bring. But he's not. Neither of them is.

Tingling starts in my biceps, like I can feel the strength

moving through my veins. With each step I'm stronger, deadlier. I'm confident, in control. The power fills me completely, making every breath I take easier, lighter.

With both arms outstretched I push Pace in the chest. He stumbles backward so fast and slams into the wall so hard, air rushed from his lungs through his half-opened mouth. Mateo grabs the front of my shirt, pulling me up to his face.

"You got a problem, tracker?" he asks, his breath hot, eyes cold.

"No. But you do now," I say and put my hands on his shoulders. I think my plan was to lift him up, toss his wisecracking butt across the gym and see how he liked it. But that's halted by Mr. Strickman, who pulls me back while Ms. Granger, the assistant gym teacher, grabs Mateo.

"To my office, now, Kramer!"

Nurse Hilden places an ice pack on my nose and I swear it feels like the room spins. It's cold and it feels better, but I'm dizzy and a little nauseous.

"Tilt your head forward and pinch your nose," she says in a nasal voice that doesn't go with her wide flat nose and thin lips. Her face looks like a piece of Silly Putty pulled and stretched over bone, twisted in some areas and smooth in others.

I do as she says, closing my eyes to keep from staring up at her matte red lipstick and huge mousy-brown curls.

"Now can you tell me what was going on out there?" Strickman asks in his casual, try-to-be-stern-teacher voice. He's wearing khaki shorts and a white polo shirt with the collar turned up. On his arm are two of those rubber bracelets that are for different causes like cancer and so on. His are blue and black, but I don't know what they stand for. And he must have spent the summer at the beach because he's so tan he looks a bit like burnt leather, which is a little freaky.

I don't answer him right away because I'm still trying to concentrate on not letting my brains leak out through my nose. The gushing and light-headed sensation didn't hit me until Strickman rushed me back into his office. From the time the ball hit me until I got my hands on Mateo was pure adrenaline. It rushed through my body like an oil spill, tainting everything inside me so that all I wanted to do was crush both of those jerks. And I could have. With a jolt I realize I could have truly hurt them both.

The thought felt good. Amazingly good.

"I don't think it's broken, but you might want to have your dad take you to the emergency room tonight to have it looked at," Nurse Hilden says. As she finally steps away from my face, the smell of her old outdated perfume thankfully dissipates.

"Sure," I mumble, knowing that's not going to happen. We have health insurance that Dad complains costs just as much as the rent for our house. But I'm not going to be the one using it. That was for Pop Pop, because he needed it more than I did.

Hilden finally left the room, but I could feel Strickman still staring at me.

"Is there a problem between you and those boys?" he asks seriously.

I could say yes, but then Mateo and Pace would be called to the office and told to leave me alone. I'd look more like a wuss than they already think I am. There's a window in Strickman's office with a stained and faded shade that is half pulled down. I direct my attention there because I don't want to look at Strickman. Not when I'm about to lie to him.

"There's no problem," I mumble.

"So you just stepped in front of that ball?" he asks suspiciously.

"It was a mistake."

"That's why you ran across the gym to hit them?"

I shrug. "Guess I overreacted."

Strickman sighs heavily like he's tired of talking to me, and I've only been in here about ten minutes. That's okay, though, he can just let me go. I didn't ask to come in here and be questioned like I'm the one who started the trouble. I just wanted to play basketball and get this first day of school over with. Obviously that isn't going to happen.

He doesn't understand you.

That's an understatement.

I answer the voice in my head without a second thought. Not speaking out loud because that would have alerted Strickman to the fact that I'm just as weird as the others think I am.

"Listen, Jake, if you ever want to talk, I'll listen. I'm not like the other teachers here, I see what goes on between the students."

He puts a hand on my shoulder, I guess to get my attention. It works as I turn to look at him.

"I really see what goes on," he says, and I almost chuckle.

Strickman has no idea what's really going on around here. No idea at all.

There's a tapping at the window that only I can hear. The raven is back. Its red eyes watching me.

Intense doesn't begin to describe what it feels like to be

caught in that gaze. In this moment it has my complete attention. Like I'm in a trance, I can't stop staring at it.

I understand you, Jake. I know you.

Who are you?

I am you.

What the hell?

"Jake? Jake? Do you understand what I'm saying? Do you
need me to call the nurse back?"

Strickman's talking and he's shaking my shoulder. I must
look like a space cadet to him. But I don't care. I'm more worried about who's in my head and why I feel so close to this
voice, so connected and so enthralled by what it's saying.

"No. I'm fine," I say hurriedly. "Can I just go now?"

Strickman sighs again and lets his hand fall from my shoulder. He sits back in his chair, the whistle on the long chain
at his neck moving from side to side. "Sure. Go. But if you
have any problems with these guys again I want you to come
to me directly. Do you hear me, Jake?"

I nod and the tissues that Nurse Hilden had stuffed in my
nostrils to stop the bleeding fall. I scoop them up and toss
them in the trash as I stand up and walk toward the door.

I am with you, Jake. Do not be afraid. Do not ever be afraid.

The voice leaves with me, follows me with every step I take.
I should be freaked out by this, but I'm not. It's like another
part of me—another part I feel myself welcoming.

five

"BUT I haven't seen him as a ghost," Krystal says.

Sasha asks, "Does that mean he's not dead?"

"I guess. I mean, I hope he's not dead."

And with those words I lose exactly that—hope.

Hope that I'd ever fit in at this stupid school with these idiotic kids and their ridiculous cliques. Hope that for just one year I can be normal enough to get through it without incident. Hope that Krystal will like me the way I like her.

They're standing in front of the building on the top landing of the steps leading to the sidewalk where the buses line up. Krystal with her hair draped over her shoulder and Sasha with her profusion of curls haloing her face. Lindsey isn't there, but that's not a surprise. I don't know where she went after the last school bell rang. But unless we plan to meet, she usually vanishes into the crowd of other kids eager to get home.

I catch the end of their conversation. If I hadn't been in such a hurry to get away from Strickman I would have missed it entirely. That might have seemed better, but would have only prolonged the inevitable.

Krystal is still hung up on Franklin.

Franklin, the local weatherman's son, the one who fell into the lake and came out with demon eyes trying to suck Krystal's eyes right out of her head.

As if that wasn't reason enough, I'd never liked him from the start. That could possibly be because he got to Krystal first, but I'd like to think I'm mature enough to have a more rational reason. Okay, I don't, but who cares. Nobody knows how much I like Krystal anyway.

"Oh, hey, Jake. Whoa," Sasha says, stepping around Krystal to come closer to me. "What happened to your face?"

Krystal turns and her eyes widen. "Oh, Jake, what happened?"

"Is that the question of the day?" I ask, praying the hurt coursing through my body doesn't come through my words. Walking down the steps I half hope they don't follow me. But they do, still asking what happened and looking at me expectantly the way girls do when they want an answer.

I'm heading toward the buses when Sasha says, "Mouse is here, I can take you both home."

"Good. Jake doesn't look like he needs to be on the bus today," Krystal says.

What does being on the bus have to do with my swollen and still-bloodied nose? "I'm fine," I say to no avail because they've each looped an arm through one of mine and are now escorting me to the car.

"Now tell us everything that happened." Sasha talks in a whisper like she's afraid what I have to say might be top secret.

"I said I'm fine," I say again, slower this time because maybe they didn't hear me the first go-round.

"You are not fine. Your nose is huge and there's blood on your chin and your shirt."

This wasn't an observation I wanted Krystal making about me, but what could I do at this point? I shrug, realizing that

I still have on the shirt from my gym class. Nurse Hilden retrieved my clothes from my locker, but I stuffed the shirt in my bag and quickly stepped into my jeans. The gym shirt was bloody, as if my head had been split open instead of just a nosebleed.

Arriving at the car Sasha finally lets my arm go, but she steps in front of me, putting one hand on her hip, the other holding her book bag. "You can stop being all snippy and just tell us, Jake."

But I don't want to tell her or Krystal. I just want to go home and forget about it. I sigh because Sasha is notoriously stubborn. She's like a pit bull with…well, with anything in its mouth. Once she gets ahold of something she doesn't let go until she's got exactly what she wants out of it.

"I got hit with the basketball," I say, then move to open the passenger side door.

Mouse, Sasha's bodyguard, is standing near the hood of the car. He turns and looks at us. Mouse has always made me nervous. Actually, the fact that Sasha, a sixteen-year-old high school student living in Lincoln has a bodyguard at all makes me a little uncomfortable. I mean, what does she need a bodyguard for in this town? And if her life is "like that," meaning rich and famous enough to need protection, then why is she here in Lincoln at Settleman's High in the first place? Well, an easy answer to that is there's no other high school in Lincoln. I guess her parents could have sent her away to school, an exclusive private school no doubt, but she's here. And so is Mouse, glaring at me with a look that says he knows something else is going on. I clench my teeth so hard my jaw hurts. Mouse knows about us, the Mystyx, but he never says anything about it. That makes me even more suspicious. I wonder what else he knows.

"You play basketball as well as any of them on the team. How'd you manage to get hit by the ball?" Krystal asks, sliding into the backseat with me. Why hadn't she sat up front?

I sigh and lay my head back on the seat. The passenger side door closes and I hear Sasha turning around in her seat.

"Yeah, you're a great player. And you have great eyesight. You didn't see the ball coming?"

These two are acting like detectives from some corny primetime drama.

"It's nothing. Just an accident. Let's just drop it," I say finally.

The driver's side door closes and Mouse says, "He will be fine in the morning. Don't worry. Put your seat belts on."

Everybody does what Mouse says. His voice is just like that, it makes you do whatever he says even if you don't want to. Kind of like Darth Vader without all that heavy breathing.

The girls let it drop, but I can feel Krystal looking at me. Every few minutes or so she watches me kind of on the sly. I know because I'm watching her that way, too. I wish I could just reach out and take her hand, that would be comforting. I could forget about everything that had happened today, I know I would. With just her touch I would feel calm.

But I won't touch her. Haven't since she started seeing Franklin. It's strange to have so much power brewing inside me but not have enough courage to touch the girl I'm crazy about.

Maybe I'm just crazy.

Anyway, I never do touch Krystal, nor do I say anything else to her. And Mouse, thank goodness, drops me off first. I climb out of the car quickly, muttering a goodbye or something, and quickly walk into the house. I don't even look back to wave.

Relationships between fathers and sons aren't supposed to be easy. At least that's what I think. Same goes for mothers and sons, but I can't really attest to that one. I just think it's generationally impossible for a parent to understand their child one hundred percent. Sure they say they do because they've *been there and done that,* but that's not really true. Because time changes things. There's no possible way any parent could have experienced everything their child has or is going through.

So when my dad comes into my room and sits at my old ratty desk, pushing my keyboard back just a little so he can rest his arm there and says, "Look, Jake, I know what you're going through," I know I'm in trouble.

Not the grounded-for-life kind of trouble—my dad doesn't do that. Besides, my life is so dull that grounding me wouldn't actually seem like punishment. This feels deeper, though, like he's about to talk about stuff I'd rather not talk about, which is just about anything. Especially now when I've resigned myself to lying on my bed, staring at the ceiling with its water stains from the leaking roof, thinking about how the girl I might be just a little bit in love with still obsesses about somebody else.

"This is hard for me," he says, clearing his throat and running his hands through his hair. It's been too long since he visited Henley at the barbershop, but I bet that's not what he's here to talk about.

"What happened to your nose?" he asks abruptly.

I don't think that's what he's here to talk about, either.

I shrug. "I got in the way of the ball in gym. No biggie."

"Is it broken?" he says with concern.

"No. The nurse says probably just bruised." She'd said more, but I didn't want my dad thinking we really should go to the hospital. He seems okay with that and moves on.

"I don't want you getting mixed up in this supernatural stuff," he says finally, and sounds like it's taken a huge weight off his shoulders.

I roll over, prop my head up on my hand and look at him. "Why?" It seems like a simple enough question but Dad takes an outrageously long time to think about the answer.

"It takes people away."

As far as answers go, this isn't what I expect. Not from Dad.

He continues, "Your mother knew about the 'curse' or these 'powers.'" He lifts his fingers to make those silly air quotes. Now I see where I get my geekiness.

"My own father was the one who said he saw something in you the day you were born. He knew you'd be one of them. I think he was talking about your birthmark but I didn't care. I just wanted him to shut up."

Dad sighs and stares at my computer screen for a minute. Then he looks back to me and his eyes seem kind of odd, more sad than mad.

"Me and your mother, we were happy together. And we were happy when we had you. And then all that changed."

I remember feeling that way. Like all was well and then… "Because she left?"

He shook his head. "No, because of that power."

"My power," I say since it doesn't seem like he wants to acknowledge it.

"She was scared of it, scared of the things you could do,

you might do. All the stories and the predictions. It worried her so much."

I nod like I understand and I think on some level I do. On another level I can feel the pinpricks of anger brewing. It's so normal to me now, this feeling of discontent, of simmering rage. More often than not I'm upset about something or agitated. I'm beginning to think that's my nature.

"You don't believe in the power, do you?" I ask suddenly, wanting to know, wanting to hear him say it.

"Oh, no, son. I do believe in it. I believe it made my uncle insane and drove him away from all he knew and loved. I believe it's dangerous and that's why I want you to stay away from it, Jake. I don't want you anywhere near what might be happening."

"What *is* happening, Dad. It's already started and I'm already involved. I don't know if I can stop now."

"You can!" he says, turning to me, leaning over so his elbows are pressing into his knees. "You have to. It's the only way to guarantee you'll be safe, that we'll all be safe."

I feel myself shaking my head, disagreeing with my dad. It's not something I do often, just because it seems easier to keep my opinions to myself. Arguing with my dad or anybody else for that matter just doesn't seem worth it. Or at least it didn't, until now.

"I don't think so."

"What do you mean you don't think so? You don't know what this is all about. You have no idea what you're getting yourself into. None of you do!"

"But I feel like I have to do it."

"You don't have to. Say no, turn away from it and it'll go away."

I can hear the urgency in his voice. He wants me to believe what he's saying and he wants me to obey him. But I don't think I can.

"I don't know, Dad" is all I say. "I just don't know."

"I'm warning you, Jake. For all our sakes, just walk away from this."

Then he stands up and walks out of my room as abruptly as he came in. That's how it is with Dad. He says what he wants, then he's done with it. I never get explanations from him. He just is who and what he is, for better or worse.

I definitely put him in the "for better" category, since he's the one who decided to stick around. Ever since my mom left he's been both Mom and Dad to me, he's caretaker to my grandfather and the sole provider for all three of us. I help out around the house and with Pop Pop, because I know my dad can't do everything—even though he tries. I'm glad he stuck around, that he thought I was worth it. So I can understand why he's afraid.

But I'm not.

I don't think I'll ever be afraid again.

SIX

My eyes open and every nerve in my body is alert. I'm awake even though I'm positive it's still nighttime. I'm in my room, lying in my bed. But I'm not alone. I know that as surely as I know my name.

He's here, the one who is a part of me. He's waiting.

For what I'm not sure. But I sit up in the bed and let the energy flow through my body. It flows like a cool breeze, like icy-cold water sipped through a straw. I feel it filling me up like a balloon, inflating me.

When my legs move and my feet hit the floor, I'm staring at absolutely nothing in front of me. And yet I feel him. I don't know, maybe it's an *it*. But because I really believe he's a part of me I'll keep referring to it as *him*.

It's time you know the truth, he tells me.

I nod, like, "yeah, I'm ready to know the truth." I don't know why but I don't think speech is necessary. He's inside me, inside my mind and my body. So whatever I think or say he knows.

To the window, he says, and I get up from the bed and walk to my window.

Open it.

I do.

Now jump.

Huh?

I turn back looking around the room at nothing once more.

Trust me, Jake.

I take a deep breath. It's two stories. I guess I could break a leg or maybe my ankle, or if I fall wrong, my arm. I'd definitely bruise my face, which wouldn't ordinarily bother me, but with the swollen nose Pace gave me today I don't think I need any more bruises in that area.

Okay, so I lean through the window, then decide I can't do it looking down. I turn, sit my butt on the sill, then twist so that my feet are hanging out the side of the window. There's a crisp breeze blowing, actually it's cutting against the bare skin of my legs and feet. This morning it was like an inferno, and now this. But it's Lincoln, and we have wacky weather all the time, so I'm not at all concerned.

Well, yeah, I am, because as I sit here thinking about the weather I'm hesitating to jump. Obviously, I'm hesitating too much, as I feel a push from behind, then I'm just out there, flailing in the breeze. When I think I'm going to crash into the ground with a loud thud that will wake Pop Pop and break all my bones, the exact opposite happens. It's not a fast fall, just a slow-motion drop. I can see myself going down but not the ground rushing up toward me. I'm in an upright position so my face isn't in danger of smacking the dirt first. And with a light muffled sound my bare feet touch the ground as if I'd just taken a step out of my window and landed down here.

Walk with me, the voice says.

Pulling my T-shirt down I shake off the first of the shivers and begin to walk. My boxers are short but my T-shirt is long, thankfully. That only means I probably look like some girly dork walking outside in the middle of the night in my underwear, no less. I don't see anybody around so I guess I don't have to worry about being razzed about this tomorrow on the bus.

In another time and place there was a goddess who ruled over everything.

Styx, I volunteer, eager to show I know something at least.

She ruled my world, bringing the strongest of gods to their knees before her.

Who are you?

I am that from which your power was born.

I thought our powers came from the weather. That's what Fatima said.

The Messenger can only tell you so much. She cannot tip the scales. She could just as easily have been a messenger of dark. Styx has control of her.

So Fatima lied to us. Is that what you're telling me?

I am telling you that there is more to know.

Like what?

You are very powerful because my displeasure with her was great. That is why the storms grow so violent. She controls the sun and the moon, the power that surges from both. Her plan was to create an army to fight against me. With my own power, I add to the intensity, the heat, the heart of every storm.

So our power is from both of you. Styx who is the light and you… my thought trails off.

I am the dark. And so are you.

I stop, right there my feet refuse to move. "I am not dark." The words come out of my mouth before I can prevent them.

You have me inside of you. I know it. I have felt it.

No, I say, but feel just a bit of truth to the words.

You have felt it, too. You like the feeling. It is feeding your hungry soul.

I am a Mystyx. We were created to fight against the dark, in the name of Styx and her curse.

You do not even know what her curse is or its purpose.

I know that she cursed the dark. She is the light.

She is the goddess of the river that circles the Underworld. There is no light in the Underworld.

My toes curl into the drying grass. I'd walked behind the houses close to the tracks but not crossing them where the woods awaited on the other side. There are sloping hills here, land not yet used for new construction. A few months back all this land was slotted to become a new club for the Richies, but Sasha put a stop to that. How she'd done it she never said, but my family and the rest of the residents nearby had been able to keep our houses because of her. I was sort of thankful because that meant my dad and Pop Pop had a place to live. As for me, I don't want to stay here anyway.

All that aside, the voice within's words ring in my mind. What he'd just said made absolute sense. But how could that be?

So the goddess Styx is evil? Is that what you're saying?

There is a blurry line between good and evil, light and dark, or whatever you wish to call it in this place. But yes, she is from the Underworld, therefore she is of a dark nature. And you are born of her.

Which meant I was dark? Or at least I think that's what he's trying to tell me.

The other Mystyx are born of her, too. I still don't get what he's trying to tell me.

They do not have the power you have.

This is true. All of us have different powers. But I'm the

only one with an active power. Krystal is a medium, a power
linked to her mind and her acceptance. Lindsey is telepathic,
again, her power uses the mind, not a physical essence. Sasha,
on the other hand, can move through space. But her powers
have no effect on anyone other than her. I was the only one
who could lift or move objects, hurt people.

You can do so much more. I can teach you.

What he's saying sounds right and wrong all at the same
time. If he's here and he's telling me this, then he—the voice
within me—is evil.

No!

*Search your heart, Jake. You hunger for what I have to teach you.
And when you are ready you will ask for my help. You will need me.*

"No!" I yell out loud this time and turn back, running toward my house like a band of wild dogs is chasing me. I run
so fast I can't even feel my feet touching the ground. Then
I'm standing beneath the back window of the house, no key
to get in. I should be out of breath, but I'm not. Looking up
at the window that I'd jumped out of I wonder how I'm going
to get back inside.

Jump.

The voice is speaking again, but I want to ignore it. I want
to shut it out for good because I don't like what it said or how
those words make me feel. Still, I need to get back inside.

Taking a few steps back I start to run again. Then I jump
and land right on the windowsill. Adrenaline pours through
my veins and I can't help but smile. It's a rush, this running
fast without effort and jumping up and down two stories. I
feel powerful, almighty, confident.

Then I slip inside, climb back into my bed and feel confused all over again.

★ ★ ★

The first thing I notice this morning, looking in the bathroom mirror, is that my nose is healed. There's no bruising, no swelling, nothing. I look exactly the way I did yesterday morning, ratty brown hair and all.

Not possible, is my first thought. My nose was twice its normal size yesterday, puffed up like somebody had put a glob of clay in the middle of my face. It was purple and bruised and sore.

I touch my nose now as I continue to stare in confusion. It doesn't hurt when I touch it, the color is normal, the size just fine. Long, narrow, a little crooked, just like it was yesterday morning and the day before that. As if Pace had never thrown that ball and I'd never caught it with my face.

The heat starts then, right in my biceps where it always originates. The green is glowing as I turn to the side and spy it in the mirror. My power. It's growing. Curious to see how much power I have, I stand back from the mirror staring at it until it swings on its hinges, opening the way to the medicine cabinet. Inside I focus on the bottles of pills, jars of cold elixir, cotton balls and swabs. They all start moving, marching out of the cabinet in a long line. All around the bathroom they go, coming back to the same place on the shelf again. The mirrored door slams shut and I see myself again.

My hair is thick and flying in all directions, my eyes blaze with adrenaline. Reaching for the drawer I grab the scissors and start whacking away at the long strands of hair that curled over my shirt or hooded jackets. I cut it so short my scalp is almost visible. On top there's a little more left, but it isn't in my eyes anymore. My entire face is visible, from the line of my jaw to the bridge of my nose and the vein slightly protruding in my forehead.

I look different, which is good, because I feel different. Stepping into the shower I bathe with an urgency I've never felt before. Anxious and looking forward to getting dressed and going to school is new to me. Breakfast is a half glass of milk. Nobody's in the kitchen. Pop Pop is usually awake in the mornings when I leave but I don't see him. Ms. Tompkins, the part-time nurse my dad hired to take care of him, isn't here yet, either. Dad would already be gone, his shift at the electric company starts early. But I don't give any of that much attention.

Grabbing my book bag I head out, walking down the street with long easy strides, no longer with the hesitation of facing another day at Settleman's. I'm ready for the day and for anything that confronts me.

Or at least I think I am.

seven

"What happened to your face?" is the first thing Krystal says to me when she gets on the bus.

She walks straight to the back where I'm sitting and slides into the seat beside me. She smells like vanilla—soft and sweet.

"Nothing," I say and look out the window. Not that it's going to stop her questions, but I figure it's worth a try.

"It's not nothing," she says, putting a finger on my chin and turning me to face her.

The feel of her skin against mine sends spikes of heat radiating through my body. I allow my face to be turned to her, allow her to look into my eyes, just for a second. Then I blink and say, "I told you yesterday I got hit with the ball, no big deal. Now it's better."

"It's completely healed," she says in a whisper, her fingers moving from my chin to my nose. She's closer to me now, I can feel her breath over my skin. Her touch is gentle and makes me feel, I don't know, comfortable.

"How is it completely healed? There's no bruising at all. Almost like it never happened."

"I'd like to think it didn't."

"But it did. I saw your swollen nose, it was turning black-and-blue yesterday when you got out of the car. From the amount of blood on your shirt it bled a lot. So how is it that it's gone now, just a few hours later?"

I shrug. "I don't know." And I really don't. I couldn't have offered her an explanation if I wanted to.

"You think it's your power growing?"

I'd thought about that as I walked to the bus stop. I'm almost positive that's what it is, but I don't know if I should tell her that.

"Let's just forget it. I don't look like somebody stepped on my face, so that's a good thing. Right?"

She pulls her hand away from my face slowly and I instantly miss the touch. My fingers tingle because I want to touch her face the same way she was touching mine. All I ever want to do is touch her, be near her. It's getting so bad my chest hurts whenever she's around, and even worse when she's away. I know I've got to do something about this crush I have on her.

"Either sh★★ or get off the pot, Jakey." That's what Pop Pop said when he guessed I was crushing on a girl. Every now and then, when Pop Pop's mind cooperates with this time period and the people around him, he gives me advice on things like girls and life. Inevitably, he digresses and says something about *Jeopardy* and cats waging a war against him. At those times I feel extremely sad because it seems like he's disappearing right before my eyes. The process is slow and painful, a torture I can definitely live without.

"No," Krystal says slowly and I have to concentrate to remember what we were talking about.

"What?" I ask.

"You don't look like somebody stepped on your face." As she talks her cheeks get a little red and she looks away like she's nervous. But that's crazy, why would she be nervous around me? We've been hanging out for months now.

The rest of the bus ride is quiet. Krystal looks everywhere but at me. I'm just as guilty because I do the same. There's so much I want to say to her, but no words are forming, no thoughts coming to mind. She's looking around like she can't wait to get to school, can't wait to get away from me and my mysterious healing nose.

Maybe I should tell her about the voice and about this surge in strength I keep experiencing. I should tell her about what I learned about Styx and the new questions I have. But I don't. I kind of feel good about my secret, like this part of the equation is just for me. I have a purpose now. Jake, the low-income kid from the tracks, can now make a difference. A bigger difference than the kids at Settleman's High will ever know.

Later, we're standing at our lockers—Krystal's is near mine this year because our first-period classes are right next to each other. So we're standing at the lockers, putting stuff in and taking other stuff out. She isn't talking and neither am I. But behind me I hear someone who is.

"Hey, check out those shoes. Are they the same ones you've been wearing since middle school?" Pace is talking loudly, coming up to smack me on the back of my neck.

Heat instantly fuses in that spot and my back goes rigid. Krystal stops what she's doing and looks from me to Pace.

"Get lost, jerk," she says, rolling her eyes at Pace.

His response is to pucker up his lips and blow her a kiss. She makes a gagging sound and the girls near her laugh.

Meanwhile, Mateo has moved in. He's up in my face now, giving me his best "I hate you" look. I guess I should be intimidated but I'm not. At one point in my life I guess I would have. But today's a different day. I'm a different person. I'm anticipating his next move eagerly.

"You wanted to say something to me in gym yesterday, Kramer?"

He talks like he's the biggest, baddest guy in this whole school. That's probably because everyone around here treats him that way. The funny thing is Mateo isn't a Richie anymore. Since his dad left his mom last year, they don't live in the big house in Sea Point anymore. Now, he lives around the corner from Krystal in an okay house with his mother, who works at the local ShopNSave, and his twin sisters, who both got jobs at the drugstore after their last year of high school. Pace isn't a Richie either, not by blood. His father married some ex-model so they have a little money but not as much as the real Richies in town. Yet both of them look down on me like I'm the dirt under their fingernails.

"I said what I had to say" is my response.

Mateo's pushing closer to me. I take a step back and hit the locker. "You're such an asshole. You're not even worth my time. I hate even having to look at you," he says.

And I know he means it. He doesn't know me, doesn't know anything about me other than my address, but he really hates me. I breathe deeply and inhale an acidic stench. It's like I'm breathing it in with every breath I take. It's filling me, growing inside of me, forming something that's making me stronger.

"Same goes," I say through clenched teeth.

"Stay outta my way," he growls.

I smirk and it feels good. I know the other kids are watching us. They've formed a semicircle around us. Krystal's right beside me, I can sense her closeness. The M on my arm heats with her presence. The other kids want to see what I'm going to do, how I'm going to react. They probably expect me to walk away, because that's what I normally do.

But today…today is different.

Just over Mateo's shoulder is where I settle my gaze. Every locker on the opposite side of the hall flies open. As everyone turns with the loud clanking sound, I nod and they slam shut. I do the same for the lockers on my side of hall. Now there's whispers and murmurs about what's going on.

"What the hell?" Pace says. "Let's get outta here, man," he pulls on Mateo's arm.

"Remember what I said," Mateo says as Pace pulls him away from me.

"Remember what I said," I toss right back at him, giving a slight nod of my head, knocking their books from their arms.

"Jake, stop it," Krystal says grabbing my arm. "Not here."

That calming sensation that I get whenever she touches me is back. It lowers the rush of adrenaline from my power. "It's fine," I say looking down at her. "They don't know who's doing it."

"But you shouldn't be doing this here. This isn't what the power is for."

She's right, I know. But it feels pretty good to get the best of Mateo and Pace for a change. I'm sick of them bullying me just because they think they can. I'm tired of the wisecracks and the pranks and the embarrassment I've endured for years because of them. Why shouldn't I be able to fight back? What good is this power if I can't do anything for myself?

Those questions race through my mind as I go from class to class. I don't see a problem with using my powers to get even, and for once in my life come out on top. I know we agreed not to flaunt our powers and I respect that, but it's time I take a stand.

It's time Mateo and Pace and pea-brained bullies like them get what's coming to them.

"Are you okay?" Sasha asks Lindsey when we all sit down at the lunch table the next day.

I've been in a strange mood, feeling like I'm expecting something but not sure what. During morning classes I was pretty anxious, and once when I looked toward the window I saw the raven. It's like it's no longer watching me, but following me. I guess if it were a dog, I'd take it in—you know, man's best friend and all that. It's kind of different with a bird, a raven at that. Still, it belongs to me now and I belong to it. Again, that's not something I'm anxious to tell the girls. Both Sasha and Krystal have had confrontations with birds, so they're afraid of them. Lindsey hasn't been fortunate enough to meet them face-to-face. But I'm sure telling them one in particular—because I know it's the same one each time I see it—has been following me on a pretty daily basis now would not go over well.

"I'm fine," Lindsey answers.

Her answer doesn't ring true, probably not to any of us. She's wearing black again, all black this time. Black skinny jeans, black ballerina flats, a black T-shirt and a long black sweater that actually looks too hot to have on the second week of September. When she stepped off the school bus this morning she was even wearing her large-framed black shades. The sun wasn't out; in fact, it was a gloomy, overcast day. I get the feeling she's hiding from something.

"You look like you're in mourning," Krystal says, opening her lunch bag and pulling out her sandwich and a Sprite.

Sasha's already opening her bag, setting her plastic Baggies of carrots and celery sticks to the side while unwrapping her ham-and-cheese sandwich.

It's kind of weird having only girls for friends. Watching their habits gives me some insight into the species, not that I know what to do with all that information. But Sasha's mom has her on this healthy kick so everything she eats is full of vitamins and good stuff. I think Casietta, Sasha's old house-keeper, used to let her slack a little. But Casietta's been gone for about four months now. I know Sasha misses her so I try not to bring it up, even though I'm wondering why Sasha's Guardian would leave her now, when it seems like we'd need guarding the most. I think it's connected to her father's and Franklin's father's disappearance, too. However, I note there's ham in Sasha's sandwich today and I wonder how she convinced her mother to let her have that.

Krystal doesn't eat a lot. When we first started having lunch with her she didn't eat at all. Now she does take a few bites out of whatever sandwich she has and drinks her entire Sprite everyday. Krystal's mom is a little more lenient in what Krys-tal eats, but she's becoming a little fanatical about the church and religion thing. It's rubbing off on Krystal, too, because now when we talk about the evil stalking us she usually brings up the origins of good and evil as learned through the Bible. The similarities are startling, but I'm not sure there's a con-nection with what we're going through now.

Lindsey, she's still an enigma to me. She talks a mile a min-ute and eats just as fast. I think that's probably so she doesn't really taste it. But she's small as a bird and doesn't seem to have any issues about gaining weight. She looks a little pale today and that worries me some.

"Aren't you hot?" I ask.

I was hot earlier today so I took my hoodie off. Meagan Helmper was sitting behind me in Geometry and she sort of gasped when I did. I haven't been without my hoodie in school for years so I guess she was just surprised that I'd taken it off at all. I just wore a T-shirt underneath it and it was a clean one, so I didn't think there was any offensive odor. Still, every time I turned around Meagan was staring at me. And not in a bad way.

Lindsey rolls her eyes. "No. I said I'm fine."

"Are you trying to block out somebody's thoughts?" Sasha says taking a bite of her sandwich.

I'd been thinking that, so when I nibble on the cold grilled cheese that was on the gourmet school lunch menu today, I wait for her response.

"I'm trying to survive one day at a time," she says in an exasperated tone. She picks up her grilled cheese and takes a small bite, chewing it like she has a toothache.

There's definitely something bothering her.

"Fatima says that in the Majestic, telepaths are highly coveted. Higher-level magicals want to harvest their power to give them a better advantage," Sasha says like she's relaying the daily gossip from around Lincoln.

"Oh great, so I need to worry about somebody else wanting this freaky power." Lindsey is definitely not in her usual happy-go-lucky mood today.

"Anybody else think it strange we haven't seen the creepy darkness for a while?"

As soon as Krystal says this I think about the voice in my

head, about what it said about Styx being a servant of the Underworld.

Sasha nods and crunches a celery stick in her mouth. "Fatima says we should beware of the calm before the storm."

"Does Fatima ever give real answers?" I ask, and it sounds like an explosion of words. I'm just saying, Sasha puts a lot of credence in what Fatima says. And I get that she's the Messenger, but she never really tells us anything that we haven't already guessed or figured out. "Why can't she just tell us what the deal is, who we're fighting and why we were selected?"

For a minute Sasha just stares at me. Lindsey sort of hunches down in her seat a little more, rocking back and forth. I really would like to know what is going on with her but I'm not about to push her on an answer.

"Are we in a mood today?" Sasha asks. "And what happened to your face? Yesterday it was all bruised up, now it's not."

"Jeez, my face is fine and no I'm not in a mood. I'm just tired of not getting any straight answers from this Fatima person. I mean, if she's a messenger, isn't she supposed to deliver messages about the unknown?"

"Well, for your information, she can only tell us certain things at a time," Sasha answers.

"Why? We need to know everything now so we can be prepared," I insist.

Lindsey shakes her head. "I don't want to know everything."

"Okay, why don't we just calm down," Krystal says looking from me to Sasha with pleading eyes. "We all want answers, Jake. But maybe there's a reason for Fatima telling us a little at a time. I don't know about you, but I've learned enough new stuff in the past few months to actually last me a lifetime."

My head's hurting, my temper's boiling now, temples aching as the anxious feeling in the pit of my stomach grows. Slamming my hand down on the table makes each of the girls jump. "We may not have a lifetime to wait! What happens when this darkness attacks? We don't know what to do or how to stop it. Don't you want to be prepared?"

"No," Lindsey is saying, and she's still rocking back and forth. It sounds like she's chanting the word now.

"Don't you want to know what's going on with Lindsey? I'll bet it has something to do with her power. Why can't Fatima just explain everything at one time?"

Krystal puts a hand on my arm. "Jake, you're getting loud. People will hear."

"I don't care! I'm sick of sitting around doing nothing."

And for the first time in weeks I realize it's true. Since the confrontation with the black smoke in the woods with Krystal and Franklin's disappearance and the weird dead bodies found with missing eyes I've been ready to kick some demon butt. We're sitting ducks just waiting for them to make the next move.

They're looking at me like I've lost my mind, but I don't care. And maybe it's because they're girls that they don't mind sitting back and waiting. I don't know, I just know I'm tired of it.

"So what do you want us to do, Superman? You want us to turn into like some demon hunters and go out looking for the Darkness?" Sasha is not happy with me right now. I can tell because she's rocking her head on her neck and leaning over the table like she's about to jump on me. She gets like that when she's getting worked up. I've seen it a couple times before, but never directed at me.

And Krystal's rubbing my arm again. While I normally like

her touch, this is a little irritating. It's like she thinks I'm this fragile kid who needs her guidance specifically. Her touch always calms me down, though, like a mother or a grandmother's reassurance. The last thing I want to think of Krystal as is my mother or my grandmother and I definitely do not want to calm down.

Both my hands are resting on the table and I'm pretty ticked off by Sasha's sarcasm. Heat pools between my palms and the table and my head throbs so hard an implosion seems inevitable. As if that's not bad enough, the cafeteria gets darker, like outside turned more gloomier than it was when we'd come in this morning. All around me the chatter of kids echoes, footsteps of others walking by grow louder. Inhaling deeply, then exhaling—which sometimes helps and is a relaxation technique I read about online—is futile and only succeeds in making me nauseous. Greasy grilled cheese and not-quite-spoiled chocolate milk isn't a good mix. The acuteness of my senses, on the other hand, is even more alarming.

So with all this going on there's no wonder I feel like I'm having a breakdown. I'd like to know if anybody else is feeling like this. The girls are still staring at me, Sasha with a heated glare, Krystal with concern and Lindsey with what looks like pity.

At that very moment I feel a hand on my shoulder and when I turn I see it's Pace. I know what's coming before it comes. It's surprising and satisfying all at the same time. I stand and I shove him, he falls back sliding on the floor until he hits the table where the Goths sit. Mateo is there in like a millisecond, lifting his fist to punch me. But before his fist can connect with my face, I lift a hand to stop it, pushing him back onto the floor.

He looks up at me, clearly shocked at what I'd done. Scrambling to stand up, he's glaring at me, then he spits. It just misses me but I'm seeing blood red now. His blood. Mateo's and Pace's. I swing and punch him right in the jaw. He jerks back like I'd hit him with a bat. The cafeteria is even darker now and as soon as I look around the windows start breaking out. Each one that I look at bursts, sending shards of glass flying everywhere.

Now kids are screaming and getting up trying to get out of the cafeteria. I turn back to my table and Sasha's looking amazed. Lindsey has silent tears streaming down her face. Krystal…she's not at the table. I turn around and around looking for her, for whatever reason needing her to be right there. But she's not.

And then, suddenly, Principal Dumar is.

eight

"suspended! It's the second day of school for Pete's sake, how could you get suspended?" Harry Kramer doesn't yell often, but when he does it's loud enough to shake the mountains hundreds of miles away.

Dad picked me up from school, after Mrs. Ratchett, the chicken-faced office secretary, called him. Principal Dumar hadn't even tried to talk to me, just simply gave Mrs. Ratchett a nod and waited until she handed him some papers. I guess that's how you handle the kids like me. After scribbling his name on those papers he pointed to the long bench in the front of the office, what the students referred to as death row. I didn't care, if he wasn't going to ask any questions, I wasn't going to offer any answers. Not that I had any to start with.

Now we're home, sitting in the kitchen. Well, I'm sitting at the table, Dad's towering over me with his bushy eyebrows meeting in the middle of his forehead, making him look even angrier than I guess he already is.

"What do you have to say about this, Jake? How could this happen? I thought we were square on what your purpose in school is."

The words come out automatically, like I'd pushed Play on a tape recorder. "Get an education, get out of Lincoln and make something of myself."

Even though this is the correct answer, Dad doesn't look pleased. "The principal said those boys reported you earlier today for picking on them," my dad says, pulling a glass from the cabinet and slamming it down on the counter.

He's probably going to get a glass of juice when he really wants something stronger. Dad never drinks liquor in front of me. Sure, I know he drinks because I've seen the bottles of vodka come and go. Not on a regular basis, but still, I put the trash out so I see when the bottle was finished and disposed of.

But I never see Dad actually take a drink or drunk for that matter. All I see is Dad going to work and Dad coming home. Truth be told, I don't know if he did anything other than that. I wish he would; I mean, he could have a better life. He could meet a nice woman; get married again. I know some people don't like stepparents, namely Krystal, but I think it'd be kind of cool to have a woman around the house again. At least then I'd know my dad was being taken care of, instead of him always taking care of us.

I feel bad that he had to leave work to come and get me from school. But I feel worse that he has no clue what's been going on with me for the last few years. That's probably my fault, not wanting to stress him any more than he was. Dad would often ask how was school, who were my friends and stuff like that. I think he had a list or something that he went down the line and asked questions from. Either way, I guess it was still thoughtful of him to ask. I just never answered.

"I don't pick on them," I say quietly.

"Then tell me what happened. And I want the whole truth, Jake."

I sigh and sit back in my chair. He really doesn't want the

whole truth. I keep saying that's what I want but as the bits and pieces roll in, I'm not so sure. Whatever happened this afternoon was because of me, that was the truth. I broke those windows out, I pushed Pace first. I punched Mateo. And it made me feel good.

"Those two bother me all the time. I guess I just got tired of it today. So when they approached me in the cafeteria I just struck first."

"Some boys have been picking on you and you didn't tell me?" Dad looks startled, then hurt, then really pissed off. I guess I should have told him.

"I didn't want to worry you with silly stuff."

"Somebody bullying you is not silly, Jake."

I shrug. "I just figured you had better things to worry about. But it's cool, I don't think they'll bother me anymore."

"It's not cool," Dad says. "Bullying is never cool and you should have said something sooner."

"I should have said what? That two guys are picking on me because I'm poor?" The minute I say that I feel like dirt.

Dad comes over, cups a hand on my shoulder and looks me straight in the eye. "We are not poor, Jake. We have all the money we need to do the things we need to do. Just because we don't live in the better neighborhoods or drive fancy cars doesn't mean we don't have anything. Besides, we've got each other, and that counts more than anything material."

He's hurt by my words and I'm made just a little sad by his. I want to believe him, I want to take the same stance he has about our life. But I can't. Not today. Not when I finally got a taste of having the upper hand.

"I'm going up to that school first thing tomorrow to take care of this."

"No!" I yell and stand up. Then Dad's stern look sits me right back down. "I mean, it's okay. I think today may have handled it."

"No, Jake. I think today may have opened the door for more than you think. I saw the broken windows. The principal doesn't know how but he thinks you're responsible for that. Now, I'm gonna ask you straight out and I want an honest answer, did you do that, too?"

I could lie to him. I guess I could. If I look away or down at the table I could shake my head no. But that seems so cowardly and I'm tired of taking the coward's way out. "Yeah, I did it. You already knew I had power."

Dad sighs and shakes his head. He's the one to look down at the table, then back up at me with a slow steady stare. "You have no idea what you're playing with. These powers are so much more than you think."

"How do you know?" I ask, because I want to know what makes him think he can tell me about a power he doesn't possess and barely wants to acknowledge.

"I've seen what they can do, Jake. Firsthand. I've watched that power destroy lives. I won't watch it destroy you."

Suddenly I don't want to hear anymore. I don't want Dad's answers. I just want to get away from here. I don't know if it's what he's saying in that somber voice with the sad eyes or what he's not saying that's shaken me up. But I can't stand it in here anymore, seems like I'm choking on the air. I stand up slow.

"I know what I'm doing," I say, and start to walk out of the kitchen.

"You don't know. Think about that, Jake, think about everything you don't know about this power and then tell me if it's worth throwing your life away for."

My back is to my dad and that's probably better for what I'm about to say. "It doesn't matter. It's my power and I have a right to use it."

"And it's my job as your parent to keep you safe," he says solemnly. "I will protect you, Jake. Whether you want me to or not."

nine

LYING on my bed hours later I can't think of anything else but my dad's words. What did he mean? What was he planning to do? I don't think there's anything he can do. He doesn't have any power, he wasn't chosen by the goddess. I was. And I'm really starting to like that fact.

On the beat-up old desk that holds my computer my cell phone vibrates. I don't want to answer it but I guess I should. I know it's only one of the girls, they're the only ones who ever call me. They probably want to know what happened after Principal Dumar called me into his office. I didn't see any of them after that. It stops ringing and I sigh, resigned to keep staring at the stained ceiling and thinking. But it rings again.

Rolling off my bed with a string of curses running through my mind, but thankfully not falling out of my mouth, I pick it up.

"Hello?"

"Hey, Jake. It's me."

And "me" would be Krystal.

"Oh, hey," I say, wishing I hadn't been so agitated and had looked at the display screen. I didn't want to sound grouchy to her.

"Are you busy?"

"No."

"Are you punished?"

That was a good question. Dad hadn't said so either way. So I guess the answer is no.

"No."

"Can you come out?"

I hesitate.

"I'm right in front of your house."

Well, I guess that answers the question for me. "Sure. I'll be out in a minute."

"Hi," Krystal says as soon as I step out the front door.

My street's really dark, especially at nine o'clock at night. There's a breeze, too, a cool one that taps the bare skin of my face and arms like some sort of wake-up call.

"What are you doing all the way down here at this time of night?" I ask instantly. "Your mom doesn't know you're out, does she?"

She shakes her head. This is the first time I've seen her with her hair all out. It makes her look older. I like it. She's wearing old faded jeans and a white Old Navy shirt with dark blue letters. I look away because I realize I'm paying a lot of attention to how she looks.

"She thinks I'm still at the church. They were having some youth rally there tonight. You know the cops are still looking for the rest of those kids from the bus."

"So the church is looking for them now, too?"

"No," she says sticking her hands into the small pockets of her jeans. "The grown-ups are gathering all the kids they can for prayer."

"And what do they think that'll do?"

Krystal gives me a funny look and I think maybe I've said the wrong thing.

"They think it'll help bring solidarity to a town that's frightened and thinks a serial killer might be on the loose."

"Why don't they just band together to fight?"

"Some don't believe that fighting back's the answer. They look to a higher being, you know, they have faith that it'll be taken care of."

We'd started walking down the block, like it was broad daylight outside. "Do you think we're the higher being?"

She chuckled. "Goodness, I hope not. But I guess it's like we're looking to Styx to tell us what our purpose is."

"And she's ignoring us. I hope whomever they're praying to down at your church is listening."

"I think He is," Krystal says quietly. "So what's going on with you, Jake?"

That's a loaded question if ever I've heard one. Again I find myself wanting nothing more than to tell her everything, to just let the floodgates loose. But I can't. I don't want to be judged anymore, and certainly not by Krystal of all people. I just want people to accept me for who and what I am without all the questions. And that's ironic, since I have so many questions of my own.

"I'm cool."

"I know Mateo and Pace have been giving you a hard time."

I shrug. "No biggie."

"Bullying's a big deal, Jake. So big that even movie stars and politicians are getting in on trying to stop it. You should say something to somebody about what they're doing to you."

"They're not bullying me," I say, and figure that at least after today they won't be.

"Yeah, they are. You can tell me. I thought we were friends."

And she says that in a voice so quiet and so, well, sweet, I feel like a total butt for brushing her off. "You still consider Franklin your friend?" With that said I'm so far beyond my prior estimation of myself. I didn't mean to ask her that, or I guess I did. It's something that's been on my mind a lot, and since she's talking about us being friends, it should be okay to ask.

"Franklin's gone," she says, and sounds farther away than I like.

"I know that, but you still think about him, right? I mean, you were his girlfriend."

"I was." She sighs. "I guess if he was here we'd still be friends."

"Would you still be his girlfriend?"

"I don't know," she says at first. "Probably not. Were you mad that I was his girlfriend?"

"No," I say quickly, then decide that if I want her to be honest, I should be, too. "Kind of, I guess. I just couldn't figure out what you saw in him. What he had that I didn't."

She starts shaking her head immediately. "There's no comparison. I mean, I never compared him to you."

"Yeah," I sigh. "I figured that."

We keep walking. It's quiet except for the normal night sounds—a car in the distance, crickets chirping from wherever they're hiding. The cool breeze is steadily blowing but I'm not cold. I don't know if Krystal is. She might be because she pulls her hands out of her pockets and crosses her arms over her chest.

"I like you, Jake," she says suddenly, and I stop right there in my tracks.

"What?"

She stops and turns to face me. "I like you. I mean, I know we were sort of thrown together because of the Mystyx thing, but I want you to know that I'd like you anyway. You know, if we were normal."

I swallow, then do it again because the first time didn't really help me figure out what I want to say in response. My heart's beating a serious rhythm in my chest and there's little bits of sweat beading on my forehead. The cool breeze hitting it makes me shiver.

"I, ah, I like you, too." The words finally stammer out of my mouth. "But what about Franklin, did you, like, love him?"

Krystal shakes her head quickly. "I don't think so. I mean, I've never been in love but I assume I'd know when I was. Franklin was nice and sort of helped me get through a rough time. I mean, so did you guys. But Franklin changed, even before he fell in the lake he was changing. He wanted things that I wasn't ready for."

I nod my head, remembering the day we found out Lindsey was a Mystyx. The day Lindsey read Krystal's mind and inadvertently told all of us that Franklin had been asking her about sex. I had a headache for the rest of that day thinking about Franklin putting his hands on Krystal in any way. It made me sick to my stomach to think somebody else could be with her. Then he disappeared and I hoped...

"He shouldn't have done that."

"It's over now," she says, then extends her hand to me.

I take it and we start to walk again. Now holding hands like we're boyfriend and girlfriend.

"Would you like me if I wasn't a Mystyx?" she asks.

"Sure," I say instantly. "I liked you before I knew what you were."

She smiles and I swear everything inside me warms up. I love the feel of her hand in mine, the feeling I get when she looks at me and smiles, like it's just for me alone.

The breeze picks up a bit and my chilly arm rubs against Krystal's.

"Being a Mystyx is kind of scary," she says.

"I'm not afraid."

"Really? We don't even know what we're up against and you're not afraid?"

I shake my head. "Nope. I can handle anything. And you shouldn't be afraid either, I'll protect you."

"You don't know what you're protecting me from."

And the minute she says that, the raven—my raven—swoops down in front of us.

Krystal screams, jerking back as the raven flies close to her face, its beak wide open, a screech echoing through the night escaping. Instinctively I push her back behind me, hoping the raven would see me and go back to its usual post of just watching. But that doesn't work. There's some kind of disconnect. A little while ago I felt like the raven was a part of me, hanging around as some sort of animal friend. This time it seems angry and violent and out for something. Out for Krystal.

It circles around us, because I'm blocking Krystal, but it keeps dipping back behind me, screeching as if yelling its fury and poking at Krystal. She's crouched down a bit, huddling her head in my chest while I keep my arms around her, try-ing to shield her with my entire body.

"Go away!" I yell. "Get out of here!"

But the raven doesn't listen. It screeches louder, swooping down and grabbing chunks of Krystal's hair. She's shaking in my arms, sobbing. I want her to stop, to smile up at me again. I don't like her this way, hurt and afraid. My helpless-ness quickly turns to anger.

"I said stop!" Yelling I look up at the raven and catch its intense red-eyed gaze with my own.

If it were possible the bird halts right there, like it's caught in midair or in freeze-frame. The noise of screeching and cry-ing stops, the air is now still. But I hear something else.

Footsteps.

Someone's coming.

My arms tighten protectively around Krystal. Her head's still buried in my chest so she can't see what's going on around her. That's probably a good thing. I'm just saying, the lunatic bird had her trembling in my arms. Seeing the larger-than-life blob of black smoke moving steadily toward us would prob-ably have her running scared within minutes.

The night had grown darker, streetlights mysteriously going out at just the precise moment the raven appeared. And now this, the Darkness that we've been leery of these past few months is coming right at me. And although I can hear foot-steps as loud as the thumping of my heart, the blob of smoke doesn't touch the ground. It just hovers above it. The top of it looks like a body, head, shoulders and all, but from the waist portion down it's just smoke, thick, black smoke.

"She's holding you back. You must let her go."

It speaks to me, not in my head like the other entity I'd

been entertaining lately, but out loud, like it's a real person. Krystal keeps crying as if she has no idea what's going on. I hope she doesn't.

"Get away from us," I say first, then think of something better. "Why don't you stop slinking around and just do whatever you came to do?" I don't know where those words come from and would probably regret them in the light of day, but as for now, the strange empowerment is moving over me again.

"You feel it growing inside. I know you do. He said you would. But she'll hold you back. She's trying to keep you from choosing what's right for you. You must let her go."

"No!"

"She won't understand."

"Go back to hell where you came from!" I don't know what else to say, I just want him, it, whatever, gone. My words have the same effect as they did on the raven, freeze-frame and the Darkness is like frozen. He hovers there for just a moment then shrinks down as if he's being sucked back into a space and disappears.

At that exact moment Krystal lifts her head. "Is it gone?"

I'm not sure how much of what just happened she's aware of so I ask, "Is what gone?"

"That freaky bird" is her reply.

I'm relieved that's all she mentions.

ten

Taking the bus to get Krystal home gave us more time together. She didn't talk about the bird again and neither did I. Her hand stayed in mine, even when we boarded the bus and sat in two seats close to the back.

"I'm glad you were there tonight," she says suddenly, then lays her head on my shoulder.

I don't say anything but I'm glad, too. It's at that moment that I realize there's nothing I wouldn't do to keep Krystal safe. She's important to me. Well, I've known that for a while, but tonight I guess it hits me just how important. I didn't want that Darkness to touch her, didn't even want her to hear its thick, raspy voice. Whatever evil it intended to do, I wanted to take it all on myself. That's like being overprotective to the fifth power.

Walking Krystal to her door at a quarter after ten on a school night makes me nervous, but she assures me it's okay. I don't know how, her stepfather can be pretty mean at times. I guess she means that since her mother thinks she was at church that coming home this late would be justified. But I don't understand why her mother would let her stay out, even at church, this late by herself. Then again, I'm not a parent.

"Guess I won't see you in school tomorrow," she says standing right beneath the bright yellow porch light.

Their house is in a nice neighborhood, and it's big with a wraparound porch and lots of windows. Her mother likes flowers, so they're wrapping around the house, too. When I look at Krystal standing in front of the dark blue door with its gold knocker and tiny peephole she looks just like she belongs. Like she should always be surrounded by nice things.

"Nah, three-day suspension and then my dad has to meet with Dumar." I wonder how that'll all turn out, but I'm probably not as worried as I guess I should be.

"It'll work out," she says, then reaches up a hand to cup my cheek.

There's that warmth again, that soothing feeling that spreads throughout my body every time she touches me. It's settling and makes me feel good all over. I take a step closer to her, touching my palm to her cheek the same way she's doing mine.

She smiles. "You're not as complex as you seem, Jake Kramer."

I chuckle because I'm not sure how I should take that. "Hope that's a good thing."

Nodding, she steps closer. "It's a really good thing."

I'd imagined this moment so many times. There were different backdrops and different scenarios, but the end result was always the same. My lips on Krystal's. Before anything else happens to possibly stall the moment, I lean forward. She sort of tilts her head up, since I'm taller than her. Long eyelashes flutter before her eyes completely close. My own lids lower slightly but not so much that I can't see the small pucker of her lips. I press mine right there and hold still for what seems like endless seconds.

Her arms wrap around my neck and mine slide down to circle her waist. The warmth now cocoons us and the kiss deepens. I don't want this moment to end. I mean really, the sky could open up at this very moment and every dark entity in the world could come pouring out for all I care. I'm kissing Krystal Bentley and she's kissing me.

When she pulls away, biting her lower lip nervously and looking up at me, I feel like I can do anything.

"I'll come by if my dad isn't still pissed off at me," I say while her slightly shaking fingers push hair back behind her ears.

"I'm really surprised you weren't grounded tonight."

"Yeah, me, too. I guess. He seemed more upset that I'd used my powers in public than about the suspension."

"Why did you do that?" she asks seriously. "It was intense, the energy in the room and the glass breaking."

"You weren't there," I say, remembering that I'd looked for her afterward, reached for her I guess. "I turned around and you were gone."

"I was called away," she says.

"Called away, by whom?" She doesn't answer right away. "A ghost?"

She shrugs. "Sometimes they don't take a number and wait in line like I tell them."

I figure this might still be uncomfortable for her to talk about, and truth be told, I've had enough of the supernatural tonight, so I don't even press the issue.

"It's cool. Everything's okay now."

"I don't know, Jake. Everybody in that cafeteria saw what happened. There are bound to be questions."

I know exactly what she's saying and I believe she's right. But I'm not going to worry about that now. "Then they can join the club. With all the questions we have without answers we can't be of much help to them anyway." I laugh and reach out to touch her face one more time.

My hand glides down to her shoulder then to clasp her fingers in mine.

"I'll see you tomorrow."

She smiles and I want to pull her into my arms again.

"See you tomorrow," she says.

I don't have any more cash on me after paying both mine and Krystal's bus fare. I'd just come out of the house the way I was, hadn't thought I'd be traveling across town. So I have no choice but to walk home by myself.

That's fine. I've got a lot on my mind, walking might clear some of it away so I'll have at least a small shot of getting to sleep tonight.

First, I think about my dad, about how mad he gets about the power. But what I'd said to him was the honest truth, there's nothing he can do to stop me from using it. I get why he's afraid, but I also know this is just something that I have to do.

Then I start to wonder about this power and the goddess that supposedly gave it to us. Strange weather events happen all over the world. How does Styx pick and choose who will be a Mystyx? And what's our real purpose? What does she want us to do to conquer the Darkness or whatever the evil entity is? Sasha found the words to the curse on the back of a letter from a Magical killed in the Salem Witch Trials. Pop Pop had history of his own to share with us and Casietta said she was chosen to be Sasha's Guardian. But none of it makes sense. If we, the Mystyx, I mean, were the chosen ones to fight the Darkness, why did we need Guardians? And what could the human Guardians do to protect us from the supernatural evil? None of this was adding up for me.

Crossing Reed Street at the corner I see lights are still on at the church. Guess the youth prayer session is still going on. Thrusting my hands in my pocket I walk by the church. It's quiet but I still wonder who's inside. I don't dare go in. Not because I'm afraid or anything, but I can't remember the last time I've been in a church. Dad never goes, and Pop Pop hasn't left the house in so long. Religion just isn't a big thing in my family.

My steps aren't fast, kind of a leisurely stroll. As there's a lot going on in my mind, hurrying home isn't really what I'm focused on. I should be thinking about the kiss Krystal and I just shared, about how I like this new closeness between us. Franklin is definitely out of the picture if she could kiss me like that.

The whack on the back of my head clears that thought effectively. It stings like something just poked me and I stumble forward before turning to see what it is. There's nothing there. Rubbing the back of my head I keep walking but I know I'm no longer alone.

He's here.

And so is the raven, flying just above my left shoulder.

"Go away," I say, and toss my arm up in the air in a shooing motion.

Follow me.

The voice speaks to me and I really want to ignore him. I mean, my brain says to ignore him and keep walking. Something inside me feels different and my feet turn the corner right behind the raven that's now like a foot in front of me.

It seems like I'm walking forever, following a bird in the

dark of night like some kind of recluse. We left the main street a few minutes back, traveling through the alley behind the church, down a worn path through the hills leading to a dense patch of trees.

Everything in Lincoln seems to lead to a forest, like the people that built the town just hacked out sections of trees and dropped houses and buildings. This is an old town full of secrets and history that kids like me barely ever pay attention to. I do know that where I'm walking, in this dark stretch of land well behind the church, is not traveled much. It's sort of like the cemetery—kids and most people steer clear, fearing some kind of omen or man-made hocus-pocus, that's what Dad says. Bottom line, this wasn't my favorite place in town. I didn't come here often.

Until now.

The raven stops and circles. When I catch up with it I stop, too. It squawks and I look around, then down. The toes of my shoes touch a rock or some kind of stone plate. Bending down, I try to see what it says, but it's too dark. On instinct I touch it, only to quickly pull my hand back as the heat scorches my fingers. Swearing and shaking my hand, I'm in no way prepared for the beams of light that shoot up from the stone, like one of those light beams you can buy at the Walgreens near the library. Spears of golden light pierce the darkness, whirling until each beam—about six or seven of them—combine into one big shaft of light that to my further dismay opens the ground.

That's right, the spot I'm leaning over that was the stone is now a hole, a black hole outlined by the lighted beams.

Follow me.

"Where? In there?" I'm talking out loud, to what probably

looks like myself, or a bird, I don't know which one makes me look crazier. But none of that compares to me jumping into a black hole because this voice told me to.

Then again, I jumped out of the window because it told me to and nothing much happened there. Maybe this jump would have the same effect. I doubt it, and that's why I still don't move.

Do not be afraid. It is where you belong.

"In a black hole? I belong in a black hole?" That just doesn't sound right for so many reasons.

The answers you seek are here.

The voice knows exactly how to bait me. I don't think I like that. Standing up straight, I'm still doubting this decision, but none of it matters, I'm going into that black hole. I know it. I have no choice.

Freefalling, that's what it feels like. There's nothing around me but air, a stifling kind of air that almost hurts to breathe. To say that it's dark is an understatement, and as my arms and legs flail in the nothingness the voice echoes in my head.

You know what to do, you've been here before.

Ah, no, I haven't.

Remember.

Remember what? He has to have me mistaken for someone or something else. I've never been down this dark hole before. This isn't something you'd forget in a lifetime. But then my arms and legs go still. They both straighten so that it seems like I'm standing in the center of nothing. My feet finally hit solid ground and that's it. I don't fall, don't wobble. I just stop. But I don't remain still for long. The tunnel goes to my left and to my right. My gut says go left and I'm not about to argue, since that's the only thing I can really trust at the moment.

Even stranger is that as I walk I know this is going to be a long corridor. If I reach out an arm my fingers will touch the warm walls, bumpy from time and erosion. It's dark and yet I can see because maybe, I mean, it did sort of feel like I'd been here before.

The darkness gives way to a blue-tinted black color that I can see through just fine. The long corridor winds to the left, then to the right before opening into a space that's probably the size of my entire house. I'm acutely aware of my surroundings because I know I'm not alone. The sound of running water echoes but seems to be close. A thin mist covers the floor, which feels slick beneath the worn soles of my shoes. For what seems like eons I just stand there waiting, knowing that he's coming. For me.

And in the next second he appears, rising up from what I can now see is a river of dark blue-black water running through the tunnellike room. He's perfectly dry, at least the long black robe he's wearing with the hood pulled up over his head isn't dripping one bit as he rises to the top of the water and walks slowly toward me.

A part of me is searching for the fear, like seriously I just fell down a dark hole and now I'm watching this reaper-looking guy get close to me. I should be freaking out.

But I'm not.

It all feels familiar, but I don't know why.

"We've waited a long time for you."

Reaper guy's voice sounds just like the voice in my head, so I'm kind of relieved to put a person to the voice, or a shape I guess. I can't see his face, the hood's pulled down low. Actually, I don't think he has a face, or not one that's normal enough to be viewed. But now every time I hear the voice in my head I'll think of reaper man.

"Who waited for me and who are you?"

His arms come around him, and again I don't see anything that's like fingers, just long wide sleeves of the dark robe moving in front of him and meeting in the middle.

"I am you," he says all cryptic-like.

It's late, I've had a long day with fighting my two enemies in school, getting suspended, having a bird attack my girlfriend—or the girl I think is my girlfriend. I'm just so tired of this game.

My frustration comes out on a sigh. "I mean do you have a name of your own?"

"Charon."

I don't really know why I thought that was going to ring a bell or clue me in to what's going on here because, really, it doesn't.

"All right, Charon, what do you want with me?"

"I want you to make the right choice."

"Right choice about what?"

"You are two halves of a whole, just like he before you. He chose, but it was too late. You must choose now."

There's that familiar feeling again, like I've been here before or at the very least this place has been described to me, this scene told to me like a bedtime story.

"What are my choices?"

There's silence. Well, Charon doesn't speak and neither do I. The water continues to ripple, echoing through the cavernous space.

"Dark and light."

Then that's an easy one. I open my mouth to speak and Charon raises one of his arms. "Look first," he says.

The voluminous sleeve of his robe becomes like a screen of sorts and in it I see a town, specifically buildings on a small street, then trees and a railroad track. The track is still active, as a train moves by steadily cranking its horn as it passes. It looks like a sunny day and on the hills just up from the passing train are two boys playing. One is taller, broader than the other with a mop of unruly curls. The other is slimmer with lighter hair.

The two young boys play, tossing a football back and forth between each other. Above, the sky is a bright blue, and underneath their feet the grass a lush green. It seems like a picture out of the past, as their clothes look different. The jeans they wear are fitted, wrapped tightly around their ankles. The shoes are high-top sneakers—what we now call Chucks—and their shirts are tight and bright white. The slimmer one's hair is slicked down on the sides, while it looks like the other one tried the same style but his hair had another idea.

Then the scene changes as quickly as I take my next breath. The blue sky turns a dark, sickening gray, huge clouds forming right above the spot where the two boys played. Beneath them the once plush grass is swallowed, leaving behind a floor of gray ash. One of the boys, the slim one with the slicked-back hair, jumps from one foot to the other as if the ash is hot and singeing his feet. But the other one stands perfectly still. He doesn't look particularly surprised at the change of scenery even though his partner is clearly alarmed. I could see how his eyes widened, blue-gray eyes that remind me of…Pop Pop.

The taller boy stands with his feet slightly spread, his fists clenching at his sides. His wild curly hair blows in the wind and his face looks about as angry as the sky above him. He opens his mouth and yells something because the veins in his neck bulge as he does. Lightning splits the clouds like electrical currents, hitting the ground and causing it to open. Through the cracks in the ground something even more familiar appears, the slinky smoke silhouettes we'd seen after the tornado in my yard.

There are about ten of them, all moving to form a circle around the thin light-haired boy. The other boy opens his mouth and yells again. It looks as if the entire world shakes then, the clouds, the ground, the light-haired boy who falls onto his knees. The silhouettes move in closer to the boy on his knees, then freeze. For seconds they're perfectly still. The other boy lifts his arms, makes some sort of motion and says more words. The silhouettes look as if they're now at attention, forming a single line and moving toward the boy with the lifted hands, the one I now realize has power over them.

Like the closing of a door Charon's arm falls back to his side. The vision is gone.

Me, I'm shaking like a thief caught red-handed. Was that my grandfather? And if so, the other boy had to be his brother, William. The one with the same power as me.

"What was that?" My voice comes out sounding like a girl's, so I clear my throat and shift from one foot to the other.

"It's the past, but it can be again."

I'm shaking my head because his words just don't make sense. "Was that my great-uncle? Was that William Kramer?"

The hooded head nods. "He was the Vortex."

"Was? What's a Vortex?"

"A Vortex possesses both light and dark powers, Styx's moon and sun energy combined with the dark power I've harnessed over time. A Vortex is very powerful. The former could not handle it. Now it is your turn. You must claim your destiny."

This isn't right. It doesn't make sense. And then again, it does. "Where am I?"

"You are at the portal of the Underworld."

"But I live on Earth, in Lincoln, Connecticut. There's no Underworld there." It sounds crazy and maybe even naive after all I've seen and been through in the last few months, but hey, I'm trying to hold on to some semblance of reality.

"You are wrong. Our world was here before your Earth. We are the Beginning and now, your Earth and your friends may be the End."

The Beginning and the End? It probably made sense, but not to me and not right now. "So what do you want with me? Why are you and that bird following me around?"

"The dark and the light combine in you."

"And?"

"And I am here to help you make the right choice."

Okay, let me just get this straight, I'm in the Underworld. Charon the no-face man is wearing a dark robe with a hood pulled over his head like a reaper, the raven led me here... "Let me guess, you want me to choose the dark."

He nods his head. "Your destiny is not with the others. Their power is nothing compared to yours."

"They're my friends," I say, but the argument sounds weak even to my own ears.

"When the time comes friends will not matter."

"I don't understand, why do you want me to leave them? What's in this for you?"

He took a step closer and the limited air flowing through the alcove seems to be sucked out with the motion. I can barely breathe now, my hands going to my neck as I open my mouth trying to suck in hot air. Charon's arms spread wide, his robe looking like the opening of the raven's wings. His head lifts, but still there's no face, just darkness.

"Styx interfered, she attempted to alter my destiny. You are the balance."

"I'm just a kid," I say through coughs that don't help the breathing process at all.

"You possess what she is powerless to control. I know that you feel it. The power runs through you, it excites you. And you now desire more. I desire the same. There will be nothing to stop us in the End."

"What's the End and when is it coming?" Anxious now and just a little dizzy from lack of oxygen, I wonder if I'm really meant to be dark? Is the world really coming to an end? There are prophecies that predict this, Armageddons and apocalypses. Many people on Earth are preoccupied with the End. I, on the other hand, never thought about it for a second. Until now.

Charon's arms lower and air seeps into my lungs so fast I lean over gasping and spitting.

"It is near. The one who talks to the dead has already been told to be fearful of the End. The others have their own signs. None are like you."

"I didn't receive a sign."

"You are here," he says simply, like that should prove everything. And actually, I think it kind of does.

Then Charon is backing up, going toward that eerie-looking water again.

I take a step toward him, unwilling to let him leave just yet. It's crazy wanting to stay in the Underworld long, but I have my reasons. "Wait. I have more questions. I need to know what to do. I don't want to choose the dark."

Charon is now holding a long stick and I can just barely make out the outline of a boat on the surface of the water. He plants the stick into the water and pushes away from the damp floor.

"It has already chosen you," he says before disappearing.

eleven

Pride—a reasonable or justifiable self-respect
Merriam Webster's Dictionary

"You're not really as mean as you want people to believe," Krystal says on Saturday afternoon as we sit in the grassy spot beneath a huge tree.

We went to see a movie, some chick flick, that had Krystal just about crying at the happy ending. Me, I took advantage of the fact that she was in such a romantic mood and finally put my arm around her in a public place. She laid her head on my shoulder and I warmed all over. Don't ask me what happened in the movie or where the five-dollar popcorn I bought went. All I know is having Krystal cuddled against me was the best thing that's ever happened to me.

After the movie we decided to skip the crowds at the mall and came here to Lincoln Park instead. It's nice here, in the center of the town where I grew up. I never really take the time to walk through this park, drinking in the scenery and all that. I just know it's here and that everything else was built around it. But today Krystal and I walk past statues of generals and fallen-soldier memorials that represent native Lincolners who'd fought for our country. We stand for long, quiet minutes staring at the statue of what looks like a big balloon and arrow-pointed rings wrapped around it. The plaque reads "The End," and I think for a minute of what Charon said to me. But beside me, Krystal's smile and gentle urging that we find a quiet place to sit erase the thought.

"I don't try to act mean," I say in response to her statement. Grabbing a handful of grass, I open my fingers and watch as the strands fall back to the ground. This occupies my hands because I don't want Krystal to think I'm a horny goof always wanting to grope her. I can't help it though, she always looks so good, so soft. She's got the perfect body, the perfect face. I'm so whipped when it comes to her.

"Well, you try to act like you don't care. But I think you really do."

We sit with our backs to the huge tree, our legs stretched out. One side of my body is completely touching one side of hers.

I shrug. "I care about stuff. And then there's stuff I don't care about."

"I know you care about your family and your grades at school."

She's right on both counts. Getting suspended might really mess with my GPA. Especially since teachers aren't allowed to give you makeup work for missing school due to suspension. That means lots of extra-credit assignments might be required this semester. And my family, of course I care about them. All of them, even the ones no longer here.

"We're pretty close," I say. "My family, I mean. Me, Dad and Pop Pop, we're all each other's got."

"Yeah, I figured that. What happened to your mom?" she asks.

I think for a minute. What should I tell her? I could make something up, but why? The fact is she's gone.

"She left when I was six. I don't really know why. Dad doesn't talk about it much." And neither do I, until now. It doesn't feel that bad, really. Talking about my mom being gone. For a long time I've been afraid to speak the words out loud. Not sure why, maybe because Dad never wants to talk about her. Pop Pop just gets this look on his face whenever she's mentioned, but he never goes into any detail. Today, I get to talk about her and not feel bad. Or at least not feel so bad.

"I still miss her," I add.

"My dad left, too," she offers. "I mean, he's still around, in California to be exact. With his girlfriend/baby mama, my old nanny."

"Jeez, that's so messed up."

"Tell me about it. They want me to come out for Christmas, but I've already turned them down. No way do I want to be a part of that new family."

"But you still love him, right?"

She sighs. "Yeah, I do. He's just changed so much and done some pretty stupid things. I guess I can just love him from a distance."

"At least you know where he is," I say, wondering again where Mom went when she left us.

"He knows where I am, too, but that doesn't make him want to see me any more frequently."

"You're still lucky. If you want to call him just to say hi, you can. If you do decide you want to see him, not necessarily his baby mama and child, you can."

She chuckles. "Yeah, I can. You miss your mom a lot, huh?"

"I guess I miss what could have been. You know, she could have been one of those stay-at-home moms who make sure there's a snack waiting for you when you get home from school. Who ruffles your hair while you're doing homework at the kitchen table. Or she could have been the working mother who still kept the household running smoothly and didn't take any mess when it came to grades." I sigh because my chest is feeling really tight now. "I just miss what I didn't have."

Krystal reaches over and takes my hand then. "But what you've had is good, too. Your grandfather loves you so much. And your dad does, too, that's why he works so hard."

"He looks at me like I'm the plague sometimes. Like he's so afraid of the power I've got in me that he doesn't know what to do. I'm surprised he didn't leave, too." Again I'm admitting things to her I've never said to anyone before. But with Krystal I feel like I can.

"Maybe he's afraid. My mom would totally freak if she knew about my abilities."

"You don't think she knows?" I ask. "I mean, if Casietta was Sasha's Guardian and Pop Pop's mine, who's yours?"

She hunches her shoulders. The wind blows and strands of her hair fly into her face. With her free hand she tucks them behind her ear. "Guess I don't have one."

"That doesn't seem right. I mean this Guardian thing, how can they protect us if we're the ones who have the power?"

"I've thought about that, too. I've also been thinking a lot about Sasha's dad and Franklin's dad. Where are they and what are they doing? You think they're together coming up with a way to come back and get us?"

"I don't know. It's kind of weird that both of them just up

and left. And where's Casietta? Does Sasha talk about this with you at all?"

She shakes her head. "She hasn't heard from Casietta and she's worried about her. Her mother doesn't talk about any of it. Sasha says she's like on another planet altogether, still going to her meetings and living life like there's nothing to worry about."

"Strange, huh?"

"Ya think?" she says, then laughs. "I don't know how Sasha makes it living there."

"She's got Twan now, I think that helps her a lot."

"I guess so. I think he's good for her. Gives her a good balance, you know."

"I guess."

"I'm good for you," she says, nudging me in the ribs with her elbow. "Wanna know how?"

"How?" I ask, lifting a hand to tuck her wayward hair behind her ear again.

"Because I can get you to relax, to not worry about all the things you don't have and to focus on the things you do."

She's absolutely right about that. Right now I'm concentrating on the pretty girl sitting next to me—the one with the infectious laugh and gorgeous smile, the sexy eyes and sweet-smelling hair. I'm not even thinking about the darker things in my life, because she's right here, with me.

I lean in and kiss her.

"You're so right," I whisper against her lips. "You're really good for me."

She smiles, bringing her arms up to wrap around my neck. "We're good for each other," she says.

Then words aren't necessary. The noises around us, onlookers, bystanders, other beings, none of that matters. Our lips are touching, our kiss going from sweet exploration to deep longing in a matter of seconds. Right here, right now, that's all that matters, that's all I can feel.

The first school day of October I enter the building with Krystal by my side. This is now our morning ritual—sit together on the bus, holding hands; walk into the building, holding hands; go to our lockers. I walk Krystal to her first class, then go to mine. We aren't near each other again until lunch, but now she sits on my side of the table, leaving Lindsey and Sasha on their side. Twan comes over joining us most days. I'm starting to feel like me and Twan can be friends, outside the circle of the girls, I mean.

I know he has his crew but they seem okay, too, and none of them give me grief like Mateo and Pace and the other jocks. The last few weeks have been quiet, thankfully. I haven't heard the voice since the night in the black hole, or in the halls of the Underworld as he'd told me. I still can't believe that I, Jake Elias Kramer, walked in the infamous Underworld and I'm still alive to tell about it. Although that's the last thing I plan to do.

The girls would totally freak if I told them, and Twan, while I think he's cool, he's not a Mystyx. I could kiss goodbye any ground I'd gained with him and his crew the minute I start talking about demons and betrayed goddesses. Still, I can't help but think about it, the choice I mean. The choice that he says I have to make. Light or dark.

I have them both inside me, and I need to decide what to do about it.

"We should go." Krystal nudges me, bringing my mind

back to the current conversation. But I have no clue what the current conversation is.

"Go where?" I ask, then down the rest of my warm chocolate milk. Hopefully she'll just think I'm so into my lunch of flat chicken tenders and greasy fries instead of obsessed with the demon living inside me.

"The Harvest Hangout," she says, giving me that look that says she might be getting irritated.

I know things like that about her now, like when she's tired she rubs her eyes like a baby. And when she's happy there's this little light that dances in her eyes. I even know when she's seeing a spirit or listening to one now. Her eyes get a little cloudy, her body still as if she's opening up all channels to the dead. It's a little weird when you think about it, though.

"You serious?" Twan says.

He did the smart thing today, bought snacks instead of braving these cardboard things they call chicken. He's finishing his bag of plain chips and reaching for the bottled water Sasha convinced him to get instead of the Pepsi he really wanted.

"You really want to go to something Alyssa and her band of idiots are planning?" he asks Sasha.

She's putting on lip gloss. I've seen her do that a lot lately. I mean, I've always noticed that Sasha's a pretty girl and she wears a little makeup here and there. Guess I just never thought of how that makeup got there. Anyway, she looks just as bothered by Twan's questions as Krystal is by mine.

"It's ridiculous for us to act as snotty as she does," Lindsey adds.

Lindsey never acts like being the fifth wheel bothers her. She doesn't have a boyfriend, so when we're paired up I always feel a little sorry for her. Not too long ago I felt sorry for myself for that same reason, so I can relate to how being on the outside looking in might feel. But she doesn't seem to mind. She's still wearing those dark clothes and avoiding eye contact as much as possible, but it looks like her gloomy mood might be getting better.

"That's right. Just because she thinks she can treat us like outcasts in our own town doesn't mean she can. We don't have to feed into her negativity," Sasha says, putting the tube of gloss back into her purse, which looks big enough to hold the contents of her entire dresser.

"Really, I mean, Alyssa absolutely hates my guts. What better way to get back at her then to go to her little get-together? Besides, the school's really the one sponsoring it. Alyssa and Jamie are just spearheading the promotion. Everybody's invited."

"Invited to what? A hayride?" I ask and Twan laughs.

"Yeah, we are not cowboys," he adds and lifts his fisted hand. I chuckle, tapping his knuckles with my own.

The girls are not amused.

"It's a hayride and corn maze. They're having grills out and selling candy apples and hot cider. It'll be fun," Krystal says.

Twan is shaking his head. "I don't celebrate Halloween," he says.

Sasha asks, "Why?"

"It's a devil worshipper's day. I don't believe in celebrating an evil day," he says quickly.

All of us freeze. I mean, literally, each of us just stops and stares at him. Twan doesn't know about us, at least Sasha assures us that he doesn't. But just the mention of the devil or an evil day coming from him puts us on alert.

"It's what you make it," Sasha says. "If you worship the

devil then that's what you'll think of the holiday. But since I don't, I enjoy all of the harvest activities."

"Sasha's right," Krystal chimes in. "Besides, what else is there to do in this town? This is the first event I've wanted to attend since I've been here."

She had a point there. Lincoln isn't known for doing much by way of entertainment. It's one of those small contemporary towns that move at the pace of a southern community instead. Generally on Halloween, the day of this year's Harvest Hangout, kids just put on whatever old masks they had from last year and went from house to house doing silly things like throwing toilet paper or bags of eggs. The younger ones did the trick-or-treat thing filling bags of candy from generous neighbors, and everybody else kind of just went on about their business. I guess adding an event to the day sort of makes it a little more festive.

"Let's just go. We're never going to win this battle," I whisper to Twan.

From a distance that she shouldn't have been able to hear what I said Lindsey nods. "He's right. You're never going to win."

Twan stares at her like he's trying to figure her out. I know it's because she's telepathic. Twan probably just thinks she's crazy or nosy. Either way the conversation shifts to what the girls are wearing to the event now. Twan and me, we just go back to eating and nodding affirmatively whenever the girls ask us something.

Just as we're leaving the cafeteria for afternoon classes Sasha passes Krystal a note. Krystal reads it and passes it to me. I open it as I'm going down the hall to my government class.

Got some new info, meeting at my house after school.

It was in Sasha's girly handwriting with swirls at the end of every letter and little hearts to dot her *i*'s. Man, I'm glad I'm not her teacher and have to read her handwriting on a daily basis.

But throughout the rest of the afternoon I'm curious. Having been getting some answers on my own, I wonder what the girls have come up with. Truth be told, I didn't think they'd been doing any investigating. I mean, Sasha hadn't said anything about astral projecting to the Majestic again, if that's what she'd done to get answers. And we hadn't had any other meetings at the library. So I wonder where this information came from.

And how it would correlate with what I'd learned but kept secret for the past few weeks.

"The Majestic 12 was a code name for a secret group of scientists, military leaders and government officials formed in 1947. Rumor was the President put them in place to investigate UFO activity after a couple of suspicious events during that time," Sasha says, sitting back against the ugliest orange couch I've ever seen.

We're at her house again. We meet there a lot now since her father's out of town. He's been gone since around the same time that Walter Bryant and his son Franklin disappeared. It's no coincidence, there's no such thing as coincidences now. Everything happens for a reason, past and present. It's just a matter of figuring out all the reasons.

So anyway, we gathered here after school because Sasha and Lindsey said they'd come up with some interesting stuff. We didn't have the flash drive from Walter Bryant's office, but we had the papers from his file that was marked Project

S. Sasha had gone back and copied those, thinking they were connected. Now we would see how.

"The government's always doing something undercover," I say in a not-so-impressed tone. "That's not news."

Sasha nods, her curly dark hair pulled back by a headband today. "That's true. But what if there was something they were trying to hide? What if they knew about Magicals back then and hid it from the rest of the world?"

"That wouldn't be new either," Krystal speaks up. She's sitting in a chair that looks like Pop Pop's old recliner when it was new. Nothing in Sasha's house looks over a day old. Like her mother just sat around ordering new stuff all day long.

"Listen to what she's saying, you guys," Lindsey says, crossing her legs and tucking them beneath her as she sits on the plush dark green carpet. She's wearing black again today. Come to think of it, she'd been wearing black just about every day since that time in the woods when Franklin tried to take Krystal's eyes.

"So there was a committee formed to investigate UFO sightings," Sasha continues. "The committee was called the Majestic 12. As you recall, Fatima says the Majestic is the land of the magical."

"How would the President of the United States know there was a magical plane called the Majestic?" Lindsey asks, looking from me to Krystal.

"You think the President was a supernatural?" I ask incredulously.

Sasha shakes her head. "No. But I think they all knew of the magical place and of the supernatural existence here on Earth. I think this committee was selected to cover it up."

Krystal leans forward, her elbows on her knees. "And how

does this connect to us? How do we, with supernatural powers from a Greek goddess, connect to UFOs?"

"There were never any UFOs," I say quietly. Suddenly things are clicking into place, like a long-lost memory I never even knew I had. Just like my visit to the Underworld. "Every sighting that was reported was real, but it wasn't UFOs they saw. They were Magicals, things from the Majestic as they appeared on Earth. Just like the things Sasha can see."

"Exactly!" Sasha says, pointing at me as if I've just answered the daily double on *Jeopardy*.

"And every time a mortal reported one of those sightings it was covered up and supposedly being investigated," Krystal says.

Sasha continues the sentence for her. "By the Majestic 12."

"Who were most likely Magicals themselves," Lindsey completes.

"No way," I say, but I know it's true. I can feel it.

"Jonathan Bryant was a scientist who was also a member of the Majestic 12," Sasha adds. She's looking around at us like she wants us to put together the pieces that she already has. Krystal and I are following her, but I guess we still need time to actually digest what she's saying.

"Jonathan Bryant was Walter Bryant's father," Lindsey says.

"Franklin's grandfather," Krystal whispers.

It feels like we should be sitting around a campfire telling ghost stories on a dark, stormy night. The conversation goes from conspiratorial whispers to surprised gasps to, now, silent contemplation. And don't think it's skipped my attention that Krystal just mentioned her ex-boyfriend, the one who even in death or disappearance is still my competition.

"And that's how Walter Bryant found out about us," I say

finally, because it makes sense. "The weatherman's son finds out about his father's past work and looks into it himself. He draws a more scientific conclusion and decides to act on it, to profit from it."

Lindsey nods. "So where's Walter Bryant now? That's what we need to figure out. Because whatever he knows, it's only a matter of time before he sells it to someone else."

"Have you heard from your father, Sasha?" I ask and receive scathing looks from both Krystal and Lindsey. Sasha just shrugs.

"My mother said Washington State. I don't know what he's doing there. But like you, I'm thinking it has something to do with us and Walter Bryant. My dad knows about us and our power. He knew that Casietta was my Guardian. I guess it's safe to say that what he knows Walter Bryant might know, as well."

"Do you really think he'd tell him about us? I mean, would he really exploit you, his daughter?"

Sasha looks like Lindsey's question poses just a hint of pain for her. But she's good at hiding her true feelings. I know, she's been doing it since I met her. For instance, she's always tried to act like the fact that her parents basically ignored her didn't bother her. She, for the most part, looks like a normal teenager with a normal life, for a rich girl. But I figure it's got to be tough for her, especially after learning all she did. I mean, how's a girl supposed to react to her housekeeper being her sworn Guardian then disappearing; her father knowing all along that she was supernatural but choosing to hide from it instead of embracing it or helping his daughter get through it; and Mouse, we still don't know his part in all this, and the big guy doesn't seem in any hurry to tell us. If you ask me, she's handling it all pretty well.

"I don't really know what he's capable of. I wouldn't have thought a parent could hide something like this from their child, but he did. When he looked at me it was as if I was a total stranger, a freak he wished he'd never come across. So I don't think for one minute that our blood ties will stop him from doing whatever he can that's profitable."

Now that's a shame. But I guess that's why Sasha and I remain good friends. She's got her dysfunctional family and I have mine.

"Fatima said our power comes from what they call a subtle eclipse." Krystal starts talking. "But Jake's grandfather said it was the storm, that big blizzard that hit the month we were all conceived here in Lincoln."

"But I wasn't conceived in Lincoln," Lindsey says. "My parents were never in this town before."

"And you're four months younger than us," Sasha says.

"The energy to make mortals supernatural came from the eclipse," I say as sort of just a gathering of all our facts. I don't want to let on that I have other information. Then I'd have to share the source of that information, and that, I'm definitely not ready to do. But I can't stop. It's like the words are just popping out of my mouth. Like…like someone else is saying them through me.

"The storms, the catastrophic nature of them, the erratic occurrences plaguing scientists throughout the world, just as the UFO sightings did, come from something else."

"What?" Sasha asks.

"We can only come from one thing, either the eclipse or

the storms. Either way it's the weather, and we know that Styx had control of the moon and the sun," Krystal says.

"No." I'm shaking my head for emphasis. "Think about it. The eclipse births the energy, it puts it into the atmosphere, but something else adds to it, pushes the energy to another level entirely."

"And by doing so it creates what? The Darkness that keeps following us?" Lindsey asks.

"A countermeasure."

"What in the world are you talking about, Jake?" Sasha asks.

"It's simple." And I really feel it is. This moment of realization is like a blindfold coming off my eyes. "To every light there is a dark. To every good an evil. To every power an even stronger power."

"Styx created the eclipse to empower us, to give us tools to fight in her place. And then, another evokes power into the atmosphere to what…dissuade us away from Styx, make us evil?" This is Lindsey, and she's staring directly at me.

Although she's wearing her black, supposedly to keep her from being afflicted with the thoughts of everyone around her, I am not. I wear jeans, tattered at the ends and faded in the bottom and a dark green T-shirt. She's looking at me or rather looking through me with that way she has. Inside I feel like smiling, glad she can see what the others cannot. On the outside I'm a little nervous.

"I think that's it," I say, standing up and moving toward the window, trying to get out of her line of sight. I don't really know what she's thinking or what she may have seen inside of me. And since I haven't shared with any of them the voice taking up residence inside my head or the fact that I'm most likely in some way mixed with some dark energy, I don't really want her seeing too much.

"All this work is making me hungry," Sasha says. "And since Casietta is gone..." A gloomy air seems to hang on her words, but then true to form she smiles through it and stands. "Let's go get pizza."

"No!" I know I say it too fast and it sounds too urgent, too serious for the mere suggestion of going to get pizza, but I don't want to go. The confrontation with Pace and Mateo the last time I was there is still fresh in my mind. I don't want to risk seeing them and having another burst of power threaten to expose us and continue to confuse me. I really want to be alone, to think about all these new developments. "I mean, I'll pass," I finish in a much more normal tone.

But the girls are all looking at me; Sasha with her worried look and Lindsey with the questioning one. Krystal has a combination of them both, worried and questioning. Hers is the worst, makes me feel like an idiot ten times over.

"I'll just head home," I say and start to leave the room, hoping nobody'll try to stop me.

Fat chance, Krystal is right behind me as I approach the front door.

"It's all right, Jake. I mean, they probably won't even be there."

"They?"

She nods. "Pace and Mateo. Besides they're jerks anyway. You shouldn't let them get the best of you, just ignore them."

"Like you tried to ignore Alyssa," I say out of spite. A few months ago Alyssa Turner had her sights set on making Krystal's life hell, and for the most part she succeeded, until Sasha and Krystal both put the braid-haired socialite in her place.

Her lips thin out a little like she's trying to hold back a response. I'm making her angry. But I don't care. At this moment I just don't care. I want to be alone, away from them and their theories and their watchful eyes.

"You shouldn't let them bully you," she says, crossing her arms over her chest.

"I can handle my own problems." And because I really believe that I turn my back on her and open the door.

"What you do affects us all, Jake. Remember that when you're handling your own problems."

When I turn back to her she looks different, or maybe I'm looking at her differently. But it's not with the softness and embarrassment that I'm used to feeling toward her. Instead it's with a kind of pity, an I-know-something-you-don't sort of way. "What I do is for me. Now and always."

Her mouth is open like she wants to say something but can't when I walk away. I don't care what she was going to say or wanted to say. I said what I did and I meant it. Walking down the quiet streets of Sea Point I feel stronger. With every step strength builds in my legs, my arms, the pit of my stomach. I hear a low laughter, more like a cackle, and I look up. He's there, the raven. His eyes are on mine, as always, and I nod, accepting his presence, knowing its meaning.

I walk and he flies with me, just above my head on the right side. He's there, like we're together, a combination, and a deadly force to be reckoned with.

twelve

SO here I am again, walking home because I don't have enough money to get on the bus. I do actually, at home in the jar in my old shoe box that's pushed under my bed. That's where I put all the change Dad or Pop Pop tell me to keep when I go to the store, and the one-dollar payments Mrs. Grimbly at the end of my block gives me for coming to her house every Friday morning and taking out her trash. But that's my Get-Out-of-Lincoln fund.

I don't really know what I'm going to do when I'm finally old enough to blow this town, just that I want to be someplace else. College is a good start, and that would make my dad happy. I also thought about joining the armed forces and seeing some of the world. Pop Pop is against that idea, doesn't really believe in our government that much these days. I often wonder if he's talking about the current government or the previous one, since when I first talked about joining the army it was about four years ago. Either way, I guess it doesn't matter, he doesn't want me to become a soldier.

Dad wants me to make something out of myself by getting an education. The girls want me to be a part of their mission to save the world or whatever they think Fatima is trying to tell them. Charon wants me to embrace my dark half.

What do I want? Nobody's ever asked me that question before and up until this point I've been too chicken to ask my-self. Now that I've gotten the question out, I still don't know the answer.

The moment I turn the corner taking me out of the Sea Point development there's a breeze that blows right against the back of my neck. I still, then shiver as my eyes search all around me. Something's here.

Not again.

But it's not what I'm thinking. A car comes down the street, in the same direction that I was walking. At first it's speeding down the street, way past the 35 mph speed limit that's clearly posted at the corner. Then it slows down, right next to me.

"Looky what we have here, Mateo," Pace says in the voice that I'm so totally tired of hearing.

It's been weeks since our last encounter and my subsequent suspension. In that time we've kept a safe distance from each other in school. But we aren't on school property now.

I keep walking, giving them the finger as I go. Guess I could have just ignored them totally, but that wouldn't have worked either. The car stops and they both get out. My heart's thumping loud in my ears because I know what's coming even before Mateo takes the first swing.

His fist lands across the back of my head and I stumble. Pace is right there to play his part, punching me in the stomach. So my head's spinning and my stomach's doing things that aren't normal or supernatural for that matter, just painful as hell. I'm hunched over, praying my legs will keep me stand-ing, when one of them delivers another blow to the side of my jaw. I feel like a cartoon character whirling around in the wind, wondering if there's a circle of birds chirping around my head as I go down. Hitting the ground should have been hard and unforgiving. Instead I feel weightless, bursts of light exploding behind my eyes.

They're both standing over me now, hurling insults, fists and feet raised to take advantage of me being on the ground. I can't decipher their exact words and don't feel any of the oncoming blows. Instead I feel the pulsating in my biceps, the tensing of my thighs. My temples throb, fingers itch as I stand.

Pace and Mateo back up, one looking tremendously afraid and the other so shocked his eyes look like they're about to pop out of his head. I grab both of them by the front of their shirts, easily lifting them off the ground.

"Holy crap!"

"What the hell are you?"

They're both yelling simultaneously but their words seem slurred and I ignore them. With a slow, jerking motion I send both of them flying across the street, landing on the lawn of another house. Turning my gaze to their car I stare until every window is blown out, glass shattering the sidewalk and street. All four tires fall from the car, rolling lopsidedly down the street.

Across the street Pace and Mateo are struggling to get up. Pace is heading in the opposite direction, Mateo just standing there staring at me. There are two trees planted in that front yard. With a nod of my head they're both uprooted, slamming down one in front of Pace and the other Mateo, trapping them where they stand.

I hear the sirens long before two police cruisers turn the corner, tires screeching, lights glowing.

Run!

The voice doesn't have to tell me twice. Turning, I take off down the street, cutting between two of the houses and running through the grassy backyards instead of along the open sidewalk where the cops can easily chase me. Later, I would think and rethink this, but for now, about five minutes later I'm running up the front steps to my house. Sasha lived all the way on the other side of Lincoln. A car couldn't have gotten me here this fast. But like I said, I'm too tired and too wound up to continue that line of questioning.

When I step through the front door, Pop Pop's the first person I see. He's in his wheelchair tonight, his wrinkled hands resting on the huge wheels. Dressed in his pajamas he looks frail and sick. If I was being completely honest I'd say he's been looking that way since the tornado.

"Hey, Pop Pop." I try to talk casually and walk past him, but he grabs my arm.

"Take me to my room," he says.

Now, one thing to know about my grandfather is that he's as independent as he is loyal. He'd never ask anyone to do anything for him that he couldn't very well do for himself, until now. Over the years I've had to watch this disease take from him everything that made him Louis Kramer, that made him a man.

Shrugging, I toe my shoes off, leaving them near the beat-up umbrella stand. After that run my feet are tired and hot. Pop Pop's already turned around in his chair, so I just reach for the handles and start to push. His room's on the first floor, right past the living room. Our house is long and narrow, one hallway that branches off into different rooms. We pass the kitchen and the pantry on our way to his room, also.

At the end of the hallway I turn easily into Pop Pop's room

because a long time ago Dad took the framing off the doors so the wheelchair could fit through. Getting close to the bed, I flip the lock in place so the chair doesn't roll back out the door, since there's a slight slant to the floor in the back rooms. I'm moving around to help Pop Pop out of the chair when one shaky arm reaches out and his hand touches my shoulder.

"They're coming for you, Jakey. They're coming and I don't know if I can stop 'em this time."

Pop Pop's words are clear and I know he's talking about my powers and possibly Charon. "You know what happened to Uncle William, don't you?"

With his other hand Pop Pop wipes his face. He tries to take a deep breath but ends up coughing out half of it. I reach around and gingerly rub the center of his back like his nurse taught me. This helps to loosen the passageways in the lungs, she said. He's usually on oxygen but gets tired of the tube in his nose and yanks it out sometimes.

"I know he tried to do what he thought was right. He tried to fight, but he just wasn't strong enough."

"The power gets stronger. Everything is magnified now. I can feel it," I confide in Pop Pop because I have nobody else to tell. "Sometimes I just feel like it's going to run me over like a freight train."

"You must control it, make it obey you, not the other way around. That's where William went wrong."

"Where did he go? Is he still alive?"

"He's in a place I don't reckon I'll ever see. No coming back here for William. I knew that the day he walked out."

"Were you his Guardian, too?"

Pop Pop shakes his head and plants his hands on the handles of the chair. With slow movements he pulls himself up.

I stand and put a hand behind him to help steady him. He doesn't want me to lift him into bed, we've had that argument too many times before.

"They only told me to keep an eye on you."

"Why do we need Guardians? I mean, you have no powers, how can you really guard me?"

"Mortal blood and mortal eyes see much more, they said. I know when to warn you, when to teach you and when to step out of the way."

The way he said those last words had my stomach twisting. "What happens if I no longer have a Guardian? I mean, Casietta was Sasha's Guardian and now she's gone."

"We not only guard you, but we guard the secret." He lay down on the pillows, catching his breath. "And that old crotchety Casietta, she's closer than you think," he adds.

I adjust his pillows and rub his back again. On the stand next to his bed is the oxygen tubing. Without even asking him I pick it up and lace it behind his head, pushing the small tubes to the front of his nose. His blue-gray eyes stare at me, then roll like a child's. In that instant I remember seeing those eyes on a younger version of this man.

"Am I a Vortex, Pop Pop?"

"A what?" he asks looking a little puzzled. "You're a growing boy who's standing in my way. Now back up so I can get under these covers. I'm tired and I gotta get up and go to work tomorrow. Tell your grandma to set the alarm clock."

I help Pop Pop under the covers, pulling them up to his neck with a weight on my shoulders and a tightening in my heart. Grandma died twelve years ago. Pop Pop's moments of clarity are coming less frequently. The last time Dad met with his doctors that's what they told him would happen eventually. Pop Pop was sixty-nine years old, his birthday is the day after Halloween. "One day earlier and I'd have been a demon by default," he always joked.

But if my uncle was a Vortex and now me as well, Pop Pop and his jumbled brain might have been closer to the truth than any of us ever knew.

Looking down at his frail body shivering beneath the covers makes me sad. I have so many good memories of him, so many fun times we've shared. I don't know if he remembers them all. But I do and I always will. "Good night, Pop Pop," I say softly and step away from the bed.

It's when I've turned off his lamp and am close to the door that he starts to cough again. I stop instantly, turning around to see if he's okay. He looks right at me, his gaze penetrating in the dim room.

"You are who you are, Jakey. Don't let anybody tell you any different."

I nod. It didn't answer my question, one of the many still floating in my head, but it was okay. This was my Pop Pop and I love him no matter what, so it's okay.

"I won't," I say, not realizing that who I am and what I am are about to be tested.

thirteen

"Can a girl really drive you crazy?"

Twan's chewing Twizzlers like they've just been invented and won the award for best candy ever. I mean, seriously, his lips are smacking and he's smiling every time he pulls one from the packet and sticks it in his mouth. The simple things.

"Depends how close you already were to crazy," he says over a mouthful of licorice.

I chuckle even though I'm not really in a laughing mood. Twan's like that. He'll have you laughing even if you don't want to. Something about his laid-back attitude and carefree demeanor that I envy.

"I mean, I can't stop thinking about her."

Twan's smiling and nodding his head. He just pulled another Twizzler from the pack and now he's waving it at me like he's teasing me or something.

We're at Maggie's waiting for the girls to show up. There's a lot of kids hanging out here, since it's still pretty warm to be a few days before Halloween. And because the place is sort of crowded, him waving a Twizzler at me is so not cool.

"Now, that's your hormones talking. See, you just haven't gotten close enough to her yet."

He might have a point there.

"You been close enough to Sasha?"

"Man, I don't kiss and tell. But I'll tell you this, some nights I do go home and can't get her out of my head. Like the smell of her hair," he groans. "Drives me freakin' nuts."

I just nod because I know the feeling. "Wonder what kind of shampoo they use."

"Don't know, but if you find out we should go out and buy a bottle, keep it in our house like a memento." Twan laughs.

I join him because that's just silly.

"You think she still thinks about Franklin?" I ask.

Twan shrugs. "Don't think about the exes, man. That'll mess your head up. Just worry about how you can make her happy."

I nod in agreement but I can't help it. Every time I see Krystal I think of Franklin. It's weird, I know, and probably borderline insecure. Still, the guy did just disappear into the forest that day, like one minute he was there and the next he sort of disintegrated. I can't shake the feeling that he's got to be somewhere, and probably somewhere close. Kind of like waiting for the other shoe to drop. I can't stand that feeling.

But for the sake of this discussion I shrug, too.

"Seen Pace and Mateo around?" Twan asks and I tense.

I hadn't seen them since that night coming from Sasha's house. That was about three weeks ago. They weren't in gym class but I tried not to make a big deal out of it. Hoping that maybe good luck is finally shining my way.

"Nah."

"You should have told me they were hassling you. I would have handled it for you."

Great, now even the one guy at school I think I can hang with thinks I need his protection.

"I can handle them."

"You sure did in the cafeteria that day."

"Yeah."

"Yeah." Twan nods and finishes his last Twizzler. "So what really happened that day?"

"Just fed up, I guess. Decided to strike first for once."

"I see where you're coming from," Twan says. "But I was talking about the windows. How'd you make them all blow out like that?"

"What are you talking about?" The question seems idiotic, since I know exactly what he's talking about. And that's exactly the look that Twan gives me. He's let his hair grow out a little, so his usually close-cropped cut now looks like he could probably get corn rows or something. The one thing about Twan is that he pays a lot of attention to his appearance. Something I never did until Krystal started paying attention to me. So Twan's hair is neatly combed, his jeans are pressed, not creased, and his button-down shirt is also pressed and not so big it looks like another guy could get in there with him.

I took a page from his book this morning and put on my best jeans. Well, I have a couple pairs of really good jeans, still hanging in my closet near the back because the old ones seemed just fine. Anyway, this morning I put on the better ones and wore a black T-shirt tucked in, with a button-down shirt that I didn't button over the top of it. Since I cut my hair last month I found that I really like being able to see clearly out of my eyes without having to move stray locks away. So I keep it cut now and even add a little of some product my dad uses to give it shine. I think I look pretty decent. But Twan isn't interested in how I look just now.

"Man, I saw you look at those windows and they all broke

out. Now are you gonna sit here and tell me you didn't do that?"

"I'm not telling you anything," I say because I don't want to tell him about my power. But something tells me he's not going to let it go.

"Okay, then let me just put something else out there. How did Franklin get in that water a couple months back? And where is he now?"

"I thought you said I should stop thinking about Franklin."

He crumbles the Twizzler paper and looks at me seriously. "I know there's something going on between you and the girls. I've been around you guys a lot these past few months and I've been noticing a lot of strange things."

"Strange like what?"

"Like how Krystal stares off into space likes she's seeing something nobody else does, then one of you asks her what 'they' said. And how Lindsey can sometimes finish a person's thoughts. At first I thought maybe I was just reading into things, you know, trying to fit in with you guys, since I'm going out with Sasha. But lately, even she's been acting strange. Not to mention people around Lincoln are just disappearing."

Oh, man, Twan has been thinking about this a lot. And he actually has very good points. I did kind of worry when Sasha first started seeing him and they both were hanging out with all of us that he'd hear or see some things he shouldn't. And now here it is.

"Why didn't you ask Sasha about this?"

He shrugs. "Figured I'd get a more honest answer from a guy."

And there it was, the unspoken challenge. If I don't give

him an answer that sounds believable enough he'll hate me and keep thinking something's going on. If I do tell him he'll think I'm crazy and maybe even his girlfriend, too. Doesn't seem like there's a win in this situation at all.

"It's complicated," I say, hoping he'll let it go at that.

Twan moved his wrist, looking down at his watch. "Way I see it, we have about another ten minutes before the girls walk through that door. That gives you ten minutes to sum up all the complicated stuff so I know what's going on around me from now on when we're together."

I shouldn't tell him. I know this, and yet I feel like he's got a valid point. If he's going to be hanging out with us—and from the way he and Sasha look at each other, he is—then he should know what type of craziness we're attracting. Because just like he was there when Franklin fell into the water, and when the birds attacked at Sasha's house, he'll probably be around for something else.

Then again, what if telling him somehow involves him? I really don't want to be responsible for anyone else getting hurt or going missing over something I don't quite understand myself. In the end, the fact that I feel like it's me against the girls, against the Darkness to save the world, wins out. It would be nice to have another view on this situation from a male perspective, and a strictly human perspective as well.

"We're not like everyone else," I start.

"'We' meaning, you, Lindsey and Krystal?"

I shake my head. "'We' meaning, me, Lindsey, Krystal and Sasha."

If his face could grow anymore serious it did. He even sat up in his seat, leaning his elbows on the table. "What do you mean Sasha? How's she different?"

I clear my throat and put my elbows on the table just like him. Leaning over a little closer, I'm careful to lower my voice. "You have to promise this doesn't go beyond us. I mean, your crew can't know. Your family can't know. Nobody. Deal?"

I wait while he contemplates.

"Deal."

"See this?" The sleeves to my shirt aren't buttoned so it takes about two seconds to pull it up so he can see my *M*.

"Sasha has that same birthmark," he says.

I nod. "We all do."

"Why?"

I don't really know how to explain this. I mean, I could just say it but it sounds surreal even in my head. "We have these supernatural powers. Something about the weather and extra energy during the months we were conceived. So anyway, we can do things." That sounded okay, I guess.

Twan's looking like I just spoke another language. "Say that again."

But I don't get a chance to because in the next instant the girls come in, Sasha pushing her way onto the bench next to Twan, Krystal sliding in beside me. Lindsey pulls a chair from another table to the end and smiles.

Yeah, she's really smiling, something I haven't seen in a couple of weeks. Glancing down real quick before she has the chance to scoot all the way under the table, I see she's wearing black capris, but her shirt is bright yellow.

"Hey, guys," she says, looking from me to Twan.

Then comes the frown. It's a little wrinkle in her forehead that draws her eyes closed a little tighter so that I can barely see them now.

"What did you do?" she asks, looking at me.

"Nothing," I say quickly, then look away from her. But I think it's too late.

"What's going on?" Krystal asks.

Twan looks away from me to Sasha. "Jake and I were just talking," he says, but he's looking at her like she's just grown another head.

Aw, man, this is going to be so bad.

"Talking about what?" Sasha asks slowly. She looks to me then back to Twan.

"He told him," Lindsey says sitting back in her chair with a slight thump.

"Told him what?" Krystal says. "What did you tell him, Jake?"

Twan looks at me and I look at him, knowing its hopeless. So I shrug. "I told him about us." Better to just fess up since Miss Mind Reader over there already took the lid off the proverbial can of worms. I guess technically I did that when I used my power in front of half the school. But that's just being technical and I'm not going that far into admission right now.

"No," Sasha whispers moving slightly away from Twan.

"Jake! You didn't," Krystal sighs then looks over at Twan.

"Wait a minute," Twan says. "He didn't just go all true confessions on me. I asked him what was going on with you guys. I'm not blind you know. I've seen and heard some things these last few months. None of you were that good at keeping this little secret."

Sasha's shaking her head. "I didn't want you to know."

"Why?" Twan asks her. He's looking right at her now but she's holding her head down. He touches her arm, rubbing until she looks up at him. "Why didn't you want me to know?"

"Because now you'll think I'm some kind of freak."

"I've always thought you were a pretty girl, Sasha. I still do," he says and I hope as far as sweet talking goes that this line is a winner. If not, I'm going to be in the doghouse with Krystal and Lindsey and most definitely Sasha.

"How much did you tell him, blabbermouth?" Lindsey says, still eyeing me.

I swear it feels like this girl knows all my darkest secrets. I should start wearing black from head to toe just to be safe.

"I only told him that we have powers because of the energy generated by the weather."

"So you can read minds?" Twan asks Lindsey, looking directly at her.

"Yes," she answers. "Sometimes."

"And you see things?" He directs his question to Krystal.

She looks at me briefly, rolling her eyes when she turns away. "I can see and talk to spirits. I'm a medium."

Twan's hand drops from Sasha's arm.

Sasha takes a deep breath, then shifts in her seat so she's sort of facing Twan. "I can teleport."

"What's that?" he asks, looking as if his mind is definitely having a hard time taking it all in.

"If I wanted to I could disappear from this spot and reappear outside or any other place I think of. I can also project myself to another place while my physical body stays here."

With one of his hands Twan wipes his face. "And you? You blow out windows and beat up bullies?"

I chuckle at that, reaching desperately for the easy conversation Twan and I were having before all the supernatural stuff came up. "I have super strength."

"He's telekinetic, too, aren't you, Jake?" Lindsey says, folding her arms across her chest.

See, I knew she was reading my mind. Gotta make a real effort not to think about Char...the other stuff when I'm around her. "I can move things with my mind, yes. I'm still a little rough at that, but it's definitely growing."

"We're all growing, our powers, I mean," Krystal says. "It's like we're getting prepared."

"For what?" Twan asks.

"For battle," Sasha says.

Then Jenny Lewis, who works at Maggie's part-time after school and on weekends, comes over asking if she can take our order. For once we don't order pizza, just a huge basket of fries and smoothies all around. The tone at the table is quiet and contemplative as Jenny walks away.

"Wow," Twan says finally. "I'm sitting here with kids who look normal just like me, but they have superpowers. That is so wild."

"You can't tell," Sasha says quietly. "If this gets out, people will think we're all crazy. Maybe lock us up or something."

"Or try to exploit us," Krystal says. "Let's not forget the Majestic 12 project. Somebody knows about our kind, they just haven't figured out how to find us yet. But when they do it'll be like open season. Some will want us dead and others, well, they'll want to see how much they can get from us, be it money or fame."

"True," Lindsey chimes in. "That's the American way."

"He's not gonna tell," I say, looking at Twan.

He shakes his head. "Nah, I won't say anything. I'm just glad I know now. I was starting to think I was going crazy."

"What gave us away?" Sasha asks. "Was it that night with the birds?"

"The birds?" he asks. "Oh, yeah, you mean like the ones outside right now?"

When he says that all of us shift so we can see out the front window of the sub shop. Twan's right, there's about twenty birds lined up on the cars and sidewalk right out front.

Lindsey shivers. "Ewww, it's like they're watching us."

"Or waiting for us," Krystal says.

I keep quiet, because I know deep down they're doing both. And they're doing it for Charon. He wants to know what we're doing, what we're talking about, how we plan to stop him. He has no idea that we don't know what to do about him. That actually the girls and now Twan don't even know he exists.

I've gotta figure this out because I've got a feeling things are about to go downhill, real fast.

fourteen

It rained all day. I mean a dull-gray, icicle-looking rain that smacked against the windows of my house like angry spikes. It was Sunday, and on Sundays I mostly hung around the house doing stuff with Pop Pop. Dad didn't work on Sundays unless he was called in, which he was today. And every other Sunday for the last couple of months. That's because people on his job liked to crap on him, too. I don't think these social wars get any easier as you get older, just a whole other set of issues to deal with. So there's these guys on Dad's job that are supervisors over him even though he's been in the maintenance department at the electric company for as long as I've been on Earth. The guys, his supervisors, two of them just graduated college last year. And the other one, he's been at the company for like a hundred years. In fact, I think his father helped institute the company. So whatever, they always need to change their shift so that they don't come in on Sundays. Then Dad has to. It's really crappy, but Dad doesn't complain so I guess I shouldn't either.

Pop Pop and I played two games of Sorry and three of Uno. We just had dinner, frozen fish sticks and French fries. I cooked. Now Pop Pop's watching some reruns of an old black-and-white on television. Ms. Tompkins, Pop Pop's nurse, just came in for her evening shift. She comes every day at some point for a few hours to make sure Pop Pop's had all his meds and is basically doing okay. That's another reason Dad goes in on Sundays without a fight, a private nurse isn't cheap. I'm just sitting here, looking out the window at the rain, until my cell phone vibrates.

B by to pick u up in 15

It was Twan. I'd been hoping the Harvest Hangout would have been canceled due to the bad weather, but obviously I'm wrong.

K

I respond, thinking of the fact that Krystal will also be there. Twan had said yesterday that he'd get me, then we'd pick up the girls. I hadn't talked to her since last night because she went to church this morning. I wondered how she was doing with that—going to church and learning to be godly all the while knowing at some point she'd come face-to-face with real-life evil.

Running upstairs, I pull off the old sweats I'd been wearing since my afternoon shower. Digging into the back of my closet I find a pair of jeans with the tags still on them. I don't know when Dad bought these but I'm hoping I can still fit them. In the past few weeks I've put on a few pounds, even though to look at me right now you wouldn't notice it. I felt it in the snugness of my T-shirt mostly. Anyway, I pull a clean navy blue T-shirt from my drawer and reach into my closet for my black hoodie. I don't plan on pulling the hood up like I used to, but it's gotta be chilly out with the rain and all.

Stopping in the living room I say to Pop Pop, "Going to some hayride thing with some kids from school. Be back in a couple of hours."

He turns and leans over the arm of his recliner. Ms. Tompkins is standing right beside him as she'd just been taking a thermometer from his mouth. His eyes roam over her stocking-clad legs and even look a little excited when he finally focuses them on me. Good to see there's still some life left in him.

"You going out with them?" he asks.

I know what "them" he means because he whispers the word like we're sharing a secret—which we are I guess. "Yeah, and a few others," I say and feel confident that it's not a lie. Twan is an other. And so are all the kids from school that will probably be there—Alyssa and her crew and so on.

Since the sun had never made an appearance, it was full dark by the time we made it to the Cantwell farm. It was south of the town, close to yet another forest border. Actually, the Cantwell house sat in the middle of a huge piece of land, half of which was covered in grass and other vegetation and the other half currently housing the corn maze we're supposed to conquer. The whole place looks eerie, with fog so thick you can barely see the ground reaching up to almost touch my kneecaps. The fog sort of matches the dark, dismal sky but not the celebratory mood of the kids from Settleman's High.

Twan parks on the dirt-covered lot where all the other cars are lining up and we walk toward the front entrance. Krystal and I hold hands, so do Twan and Sasha. Lindsey is there but she's back to her freaky quiet mode with her jeans and black hoodie on and black-and-white chullo hat. I don't know what she looks like this time, just that it's so weird the normally chatty Lindsey is turning into a sullen Goth impersonator.

Behind me some girl shrieks, and as I turn I see it's Olivia Danville, captain of the cheerleading team, giggling and cuddling up with Pierce Haynes, the captain of the football team. Their teaming up is the biggest cliché of the town.

"Let's do the hayride first," Sasha suggests after we've walked through the front gates.

"Don't you all look cute. Coupled up and everything." Alyssa's snide voice breaks through our conversation. "Well, except for her," she says, directing her comments in Lindsey's direction.

She'd walked up behind Sasha, squeezing between her and Lindsey so that she and Jamie Griffin were now right in the middle of the circle we'd unintentionally formed.

"I see two like creatures have found each other," she says, looking at me and Krystal.

"And I see no creature has been able to stomach you yet, hence the reason you're alone tonight," Krystal shoots back.

Jamie Griffin, a Richie with long honey-blond curls that look alarmingly like Camy Sherwood's, Alyssa's former side-kick, gives Krystal a dirty look.

"Let's just go," Lindsey says, not looking at any of the girls but off toward the corn maze.

In the center between the maze and the pumpkin patch and veggie garden are two huge tents where hot apple cider and candy and caramel apples are being sold. There are some other things over there, but so far all I've seen anyone walk away with are the apples and cider. We're standing a few feet from there, contemplating where to go next.

"Don't forget I'm in charge here tonight, so no funny busi-ness," Alyssa says, eyeing each of us.

I wonder if, like Twan, she's seen or heard strange things from us before. Something about the way she's looking at all of us, accusing us, makes me think she has.

"There's something funnier than this whole Halloween show you've set up?" Twan asks, then laughs, which makes Sasha laugh. Krystal joins in, I think just because she can see it's pissing Alyssa off.

"Lindsey's right," I say to stop this uncomfortable scene. "Let's just go."

As I start to walk the others follow me, except for Alyssa and Jamie. They stay behind, staring at us probably. I say that because that's how I feel, all jittery like I'm on a stage in front of hundreds of people and somebody just pulled my pants down. I guess you could say I feel like I'm being watched. It's eerie. Creeping me out more than the tall stale corn husks that make up the corn maze.

We stand in a crowded bunch that serves as the line to board the tractor trucks pulling beds of hay. Krystal threads her arm through mine as I stand with my hands in my pocket. The girls seem excited about the night's activities. Me and Twan, we just go with the flow.

Our turn comes quickly enough and we all take the three skinny steps up to the flatbed where we find seats on bales of hay. Krystal and I sit next to each other with Twan and Sasha right across from us on the middle row of hay and Lindsey right beside Krystal. A lot of the girls are giggling and shrieking, as it's pretty dark out here and the path ahead of us isn't lighted. Guys are taking full advantage of the dark, making growling and ghoulish sounds. I guess if I relax a bit I could find the fun in this, too.

The tractor gets started with a loud engine and some bumps along the road. As we ride more of the guys start to tell ghost stories.

"Really, this one is true," Pierce is saying. "My grandparents used to tell me this one, said it happened right here in Lincoln."

I don't know why but his words pique my interest, and as Krystal settles her head on my shoulder and I pull her even closer to me, I'm listening intently.

"A long, long time ago, this town used to be nothing but forests and hills. There was Main Street and a couple of log-cabin houses, but that was all. In one of the houses, the one all the way at the end of the town, they say a witch lived."

Krystal goes still beside me. Lindsey had already stiffened, since the house at the end of Lincoln's town limits is the one she now lives in with Mrs. Hampton. I can't see Sasha's expression real good but I know she's listening, too.

"So this witch, she had a lot of freaky powers, like she could bring dead people back to life and she could command spirits to walk the Earth. So on the night of the autumn equinox—"

"The what? You sure this is a true story, Haynes? Sounds like you're making this up." One of the other jocks started laughing but a few others shushed him.

"You're such a goof. If you paid any attention in science class, the autumn equinox is the one day of the year when there's equal night and day hours all over the Earth."

The jock was right, I guess they aren't all about sports and girls after all.

"Anyway, on this night the witches have unlimited power, so this witch unleashed like a whole army of demons and they all hid in the forests so even after the equinox they wouldn't be seen."

"Ooh, demons living in Lincoln," somebody says.

Another girl makes a squealing sound.

"And even after the town like came into the twentieth century and got real roads and houses and cars and stuff, some still believe the demons are living right here with us."

My stomach turns with that thought, my temples starting to throb lightly.

"He's making that up," Krystal whispers.

"But what if he's not?" Sasha asks.

We continue the ride in silence, none of us really wanting to talk about what we'd just heard. Me, I'm thinking about every word Pierce just said. The Haynes family has been in Lincoln forever, they're actually one of the richest families here. I heard my dad talking to Pop Pop once and they were wondering why the family had never left this small town. Now I'm wondering why, too.

The hayride was finally over and I helped Krystal down.

"To the corn maze!" somebody behind me yelled.

And with a shrug our little group followed.

Two seniors, who I recognize from Settleman's but don't know their names, are passing out maps of checkpoints to be found in the maze and tiny flashlights. Krystal grabs one for us and Sasha and Lindsey grab one, too. Twan and I are just along for the ride.

About ten minutes and dozens of curves and turns and dead ends later Lindsey yells, "Here's checkpoint one!"

We all follow behind her using the pen on a string tied to a pole to mark our maps.

"Great," Twan sighs. "Only nineteen more to go."

"Oh, hush," Sasha says, elbowing him playfully in the ribs. "It's fun."

"Sure it is," I say, then move a safe distance from Krystal and her elbow.

Deeper into the maze the sky is completely dark now, a

chilly breeze blowing just enough to make the corn husks sway and crackle. Around us I hear other kids chatting and laughing as they go along their own paths through the maze. My shoes are squishing against the soggy ground, making a slapping sound that's getting on my nerves. The atmosphere seems laid back, seasonal, fun. But then there's something else. It's in the air and as it tickles over my skin I think I know exactly what it is.

Lindsey keeps looking back at me, then around all of us like she feels it, too. If we were alone I'd just ask her what she knew, because I'm tired of feeling like she's reading my mind already. I'm also tired of holding the secret of Charon and my visit to the Underworld.

Last night, after I hung up the phone with Krystal—we did that now, talked on the phone for long periods about everything and nothing and sometimes just listening to each other breathe—anyway, after I hung up I felt like crap. Krystal had just told me all about why she doesn't really like her stepfather and now she thinks he's keeping something from her mother. She's confiding in me and I'm lying to her. It didn't seem right. I plan to tell her everything. Soon.

Just as we turn another corner there's a lot of rustling and we all stop, looking to our left where the noise is coming from. Barreling through the husks come Mateo, Pace and a few other jocks they hang with.

"Jerks," Twan says, then grabs Sasha's hand to keep walking.

I don't say anything but follow Twan with Krystal right beside me. Lindsey's in front of Twan but she stops.

"Anger." She starts to talk, her voice soft compared to the

laughing and jostling coming from the jocks behind us. "Dark and putrid. It's so angry, ready to strike."

Feel it. Own it.

The voice echoes in my head right behind Lindsey's words.

"Lindsey, are you okay?" Sasha asks, reaching out for Lindsey's arm.

"No!" Lindsey yells. "Don't touch me!" She lifts her hands to cover her ears, or more likely the flaps of the hat that hang down over her ears.

Sasha jumps back just as Krystal is yanked away. Her fingers slip through mine as I turn to see where she's going. All around the wind starts to blow, the icy rain from earlier returning to fall in quick sheets.

"Come here, sexy." I can hear Pace talking. "You can walk with me."

I can just barely see him dragging Krystal along. She's trying to fight him off, her feet slipping over the muddy ground.

"Leave her alone!" I yell and head in their direction, but I'm quickly stopped. Actually, I'm knocked back with such force I fall into Sasha and Twan, all three of us hitting the ground.

"He's here." Lindsey's above us whispering. Her lips are chattering, rain dripping from her face. "He's here for Jake."

As I struggle to stand up, the rain pelting my face grows painful. It's not rain anymore but hail. Dropping against the ground with loud plops, it attacks. I don't see Krystal anymore but I can hear her screaming. The sound pierces through the dark night, stabbing into my heart.

Lindsey's still chanting, but Sasha and Twan are quickly at my side.

"What's going on, Jake?" Twan asks.

"Where's Krystal?" Sasha says. "Something's not right."

I'm already shaking my head. Sasha's words are an understatement.

"It's here," I say, echoing Lindsey.

Twan grabs Sasha, pulling her closer to his side. "What's here?"

"He that brings the darkness," I say, but it doesn't sound like my voice, at least not to me.

I'm taking steps forward, not really knowing where I'm going or what I plan to do once I get there. Corn stalks are bending and blocking my path but I just push through them. Hail's falling all over, like somebody in the heavens opened a huge box of marbles and dumped them all out. The wind has this hissing sound, but all I know is I've got to stop it.

Through the storm I see spirals of black coming up from the ground. The silhouettes of darkness I've seen before. Just as I see them I hear screeching from above. My raven is here.

What I don't see or hear anymore is Krystal.

Where is she?

You do not need her. I have all that you need.

No.

Come to me.

No.

I am the one who understands you. I am the one who can save you.

"No!" I yell. Holding my head back I look to the sky, hail smacking me in the face, wind ripping through my clothes. "No!"

Fight it you cannot. You will not win!

As if in response to my cry, a funnel appears right beneath my feet. I'm no longer on the ground. Swept up in the center of this…vortex, I'm being lifted. Power seeps through every pore of my body and I feel like my bones are cracking, my skin stretching to accommodate its force.

Bright streaks of lightning break through the monotonous darkness of the sky. In the distance I hear more yelling and screaming but I'm trapped here, inside this storm of my own making. It's gray all around me and I'm spinning, spinning, out of control. When I finally fall to the ground, landing on my feet but bending at the knees, I no longer feel like me. I am no longer Jake.

Looking up, I quickly spot Pace still dragging Krystal, trying to get out of the corn maze. I take off running, my feet barely touching the ground. Coming up on them quickly I grab Krystal out of his grasp, tossing her to the ground. Pace turns to me ready for a fight. Then something in his eyes changes and he backs away. I move forward, reaching for him, grabbing him and throwing him far. He crashes to the ground with a sickening thump and I'm about to leap toward him again. A hand on my arm stops me.

"Jake," Krystal says.

My neck cracks as I turn to see her tear-streaked face. Her hair's a streaming mass of black, blowing behind her in the horrific wind.

"Let me go," I say through gritted teeth.

"No," she says holding me tighter.

I grab her wrist, the one of the hand holding me. I see the pain etch across her face but I can't stop it. "Let me go," I say again. And it's in that strange, deep voice that I seem to own but don't recognize.

Her fingers unclench from my arm, and when I let her wrist go she stumbles backward. I don't think another instant, just turn and run.

I don't know where I'm going. I don't know who I am. I feel so different. Stronger, more powerful than ever before. Around me everything is chaos but I'm in control. Of me and what I do, I am in control.

I'm through the corn maze now, kids all around me are running to cars, cars are streaking out of the parking lot. The cider and apples stand has blown away, sending apples and pumpkins rolling all along the ground. I look around once more and stop dead in my tracks.

At the end of the parking lot is a lady, a billowing dress of all white rippling around her. She looks familiar, and I hear her calling my name.

"You must fight him, Jake. He'll kill you just like he killed William."

Emotion slams into me with vicious force. A tirade of feelings: joy, hurt, confusion, elation, pain, sorrow. I can't stop one to keep the other, can't move to claim either. But it's her. After all this time, all this wondering and longing, it's her.

"Mom," I whisper and take a step closer.

But when I get there and reach out to touch her, she disappears.

And so does all the commotion around me. Everything has stopped. The wind. The hail. The screaming. There's nothing.

Just me.

And the power that has me crumpling to the ground.

fifteen

Strength—one regarded as embodying or affording force or firmness
Merriam Webster's Dictionary

I wake up staring at the chipped ceiling of my room. My chest feels like something's sitting on me, and when I move my tongue around inside my mouth it feels like I swallowed a handful of cotton. The rest of my body is protesting, every joint and ligament screaming in agony. The urge to moan is great but I have no idea who's in the room with me so I'll refrain.

How did I get here?

The last I remember I was at the corn maze. Well, running out of it, then I collapsed in the parking lot. After I saw her. My mother, I mean.

It had been ten years since I'd seen her and yet she looked exactly the same. I guess my last memory of her would logically be the more lasting one. Her hair was still long and shiny, the color of wheat, and her skin still looked smooth, like ivory. Gray eyes stared at me with that sympathetic and caring look she'd always had. And when she reached her arms out to me I could see the blunt cut of her clear-coated nails. The ache in my chest increased until breathing felt more like a chore than necessity.

Where had she come from? Where had she been all these years? Where was she now?

Mom. I said her name in my head, wondering if that's where she'd been all along and if she'd answer me. I never used to be the sort to talk to myself or believe that I could answer myself. But now, now, I guess I'm willing to give it a shot. Anything that will bring her back. Just for another few minutes so I can ask her why. Why she left. Why she didn't love me enough to stay. Why weren't Dad and I enough for her. And how she knew about Uncle William.

My eyes fill with tears I've been holding back for the longest time. I will them not to fall, to stay put. I'm almost sixteen years old, there's no use in crying over things I can't change. Especially not now.

Still, when I inhale slowly, praying the weight in my chest will let the oxygen through, I can smell her. Like vanilla and Fruit Loops, those are the scents I associate with my mother. The woman who gave birth to me but left me just the same.

"You need to tell him the truth."

I hear the voice but it doesn't really startle me. I'd sensed I wasn't alone.

"Shhh."

"I won't shhh. It's time." There was a gravelly cough that sounded a lot like it brought up more than I cared to think about.

Through the fogginess in my brain that was still compiling the events of the night I can hear my dad and Pop Pop talking. They're talking about me and over me like I'm not even here. I guess if I acted like I was among the land of the living they'd acknowledge me. So with a little effort and a small amount of aching I sit up in my bed. Turning to let my feet hang off the side I look up at the two of them, standing in the middle of my bedroom like I'd summoned them here.

"Tell me what?"

"You're up. Good boy," Pop Pop says, coming to sit on the bed beside me. He lifts a hand and grabs my chin with his shaking fingers. "You look fine, too. Been through a lot, though. More to come I'm afraid."

He's talking in those riddles again. Like he's reading from a page in a book but only reading every other sentence or so. I get the meaning but don't understand why he's saying it to me. I have to agree with him though, I think it's time they told me the truth.

"You said Mom left," I accuse my dad. "If she left why'd she come back tonight?"

"Told you so," Pop Pop says, letting his hands fall back in his lap.

Dad looks beyond tired, his shoulders are drooping as he takes a seat in my wobbly desk chair. Leaning forward he rests his arms on his knees and looks up at me reluctantly. "She was killed," he says finally.

"By who? Why?" I want to know everything right now because if I do then maybe I won't feel so lost and unwanted anymore. Maybe, for once in my life, I'll feel like I belong somewhere and to someone who wanted and loved me.

"Jake, you don't understand how this other world works. You have no idea what they can take from you, what they're asking of you. And it's not fair, dammit! They have no right. Not to her and certainly not to you."

"The longer I don't know the worse it's going to be. I'm being pulled in so many directions now I don't know what to do." That's the closest I've come to admitting to anyone that Charon's seducing me to the Underworld. The minute the words are out I feel invaded, like my words are no longer my own.

"She had that same mark you have. It was the first thing I saw when I met her in high school. It was still hot out and she'd worn this shirt with two thin straps over her shoulders. On her right shoulder blade there it was. An *M*. I stared at it for a long time. So long my friend Eddie thought I was looking at her butt," he says with an absent chuckle.

Pop Pop laughs. "Probably was looking at that, too."

My dad looking at my mom's butt, please just gouge my eyes out before giving me that visual again.

"Cecelia was like a shining star in that old school. She was the prettiest and the smartest and she didn't care what anybody thought about her, she knew she was special. One day, she told me just how special she was. Well, she showed me when she held light in the palm of her hand."

"Mom was a Mystyx," I say, finally digesting what he'd said. "She had power and that's why I have it."

"You have it because the goddess saw fit to give it to you," Pop Pop corrects. "It's not hereditary, but a gift chosen with the utmost care."

"I thought you said anyone who got pregnant during a storm, the kids would have the power."

"She controls the storm."

"By herself?" I ask, because Charon said he had some doing in the storms as well. And what happened tonight, the hail and the wind and rain, that was definitely Charon's doing, the tinge of evil in the air was definitely his leftover energy.

Pop Pop looks to my dad, who just sighs.

"There's good and evil, Jake. And there's a curse that's traveled through the realms of time, landing smack in the middle of Earth. These creatures don't care who they hurt in this tug of war they've created, they're fighting a war that will never end. As long as there's free will there will be good and evil. No one more powerful than the other, both just occupying space in this atmosphere."

"That's not true," Pop Pop interjects. "The balance can be tipped and that's what he was trying to do. To tip the scales in his favor. In the favor of evil. Now, only a Vortex can do that. You are one of few left in this world," he tells me.

"But isn't the goddess evil, too? I mean her river circled the Underworld, that's like the home of all evil."

"We'll never understand their world, Jake. Because we're not a part of it."

"He is," Pop Pop says adamantly. "You can't bring him to this earthly world because that's where you're from. He's a part of both."

"How can that be?" I ask. "How can I be supernatural and human?"

"You're special."

Dad sighs. "I'm not debating that issue, Pop."

"My brother was special, too, he had the power. But he didn't fully understand what his power was and how it could affect the entire world, not just this world but theirs, too. There aren't many Vortexes but he needs one on his side, he needs to claim you to fight her."

My head's reeling with what I'm hearing. "He, meaning Charon." I look at Pop Pop. "I've met him already, so I know exactly who he is. He needs me to join ranks with him to fight against the goddess Styx. But Styx chose me to be a Mystyx to fight on her side. Is that about right?"

Dad's nodding, his eyes looking more somber by the minute. "Why can't we just deal with things like puberty and failing Chemistry? This is not the way I intended for you to spend your teenage years."

I shrug. "If I could have chosen I'm sure I would have selected the normal button, too, Dad. But what am I supposed to do now?"

"You have to pick a side, Jakey," Pop Pop says solemnly. "Good or evil."

"Your mother vowed to protect you from him, to even use her power to cover you with light that would forever hide you from him," Dad says. "But he found out and he killed her for her efforts. She always said he'd destroy anyone who tried to keep you from him. But I don't care, I won't let him get you too, Jake. I just couldn't stand it if I lost you, too."

The hug from Dad takes me by surprise, but I have to admit his husky arms wrapping around me feel kind of good. For just the time that he holds me I feel protected and safe, like Charon or nobody else can touch me.

In the back of my mind there's a chuckle, and I know that my previous thought's just wishful thinking.

Charon is here and he's waiting. If I choose the Mystyx I'll end up dead, like Uncle William and my mom. If I choose Charon and the Underworld...I don't even want to think about that.

I don't know what I'm doing here. It's late and it's starting to rain again. I'm shivering, my teeth clattering as I stand here looking up at her bedroom window. The same window she'd broken out a few months back when she thought the dead people she could communicate with were trying to attack her. Somebody, somewhere was on my side because there's a huge tree in her yard that—guess what?—has a branch that hangs really close to her window. Without another thought I'm climbing up the tree. Haven't done this in years but it seems just like riding a bike.

When I decided to leave my house and walk all the way over here I don't really know. But I'm here and I want to see Krystal, to hear that no matter how confused I am or how much is going on, we're still together like a normal couple. Remembering the events of the night I don't know if she's going to be very receptive to my presence, especially considering the time and the fact that I'm about to tap on her window like some teenage stalker. Actually, that's not funny, since Krystal was kind of being stalked by one of our teachers who wanted her to join his porn ring, but we try to keep that in the past.

Tapping on her window feels weird. I wonder if she'll think I'm a ghost. I know she says she ignores them sometimes, especially in the middle of the night. Hopefully she won't ignore me. Otherwise I'm out here on this limb freezing my butt off for nothing. Waiting a few minutes, I note the breeze blowing and the swaying of this tree. I probably should have called her cell phone to at least wake her up. This whole trip was impromptu, initiated by the deep-seated loneliness I'd felt when I woke up. After the fretful sleep I'd fallen into with the newfound information I had, it was no wonder.

Just as I was about to give up and walk back home I hear the latch to the window. Looking up I see that she's pushed the curtains aside.

"What are you doing?" she whispers when she gets the

window opened. "Why are you out there in the tree at two in the morning?"

Good questions, both of them. Shrugging was not a good answer, but she waved me inside anyway.

I've been in her room a couple of times before, but always with Sasha and usually with the door open. And each time was before Krystal and I went from being fellow Mystyx to boyfriend and girlfriend.

It feels different even though it looks the same. She'd switched on the Betty Boop lamp beside her bed so there was a dim light throughout.

Her door was closed, the sheets on her twin-size bed ruffled. But the most different thing was Krystal. I've seen her in several outfits, casual jeans and T-shirt, dressy for the dance at school and even in a bathing suit at the pool. But never like this. Never in this…I don't know what exactly to call it. Whatever it is it's very short, showing off all her cream-colored legs. Her arms are out and her hair's in a messy ponytail. She looks unkempt but sexy. So like I said before, it feels different this time.

"What's going on? Why are you here at this time of night?" she asks, going to her bed and plopping down.

I don't know if I should follow her and sit beside her on the bed, where she looks all soft and dreamy, or if I should keep as much distance between us as I possibly can. Fool that I am, moving closer wins out and I sit on the edge of her bed just an arm's length away from her.

"Wanted to talk about tonight," I say. "I'm really sorry about grabbing you like that."

She sighs and waves a hand as if to say don't worry about it. "I can't stop thinking about it. What do you think happened out there? Lindsey's a wreck. I tried calling her when I got home but Mrs. Hampton said she was already sleeping. I doubt that, since she was so worked up on the ride home."

I don't even remember the ride home. Dad said Twan and the others dropped me off, dragging me to the door and waiting for him to answer. They must have scooped me up from the parking lot.

"It's following me," I tell her because I feel like I can trust her. Even if I can't tell the others, I can definitely tell Krystal.

"What's following you?"

"The bird."

She waves a hand as to dismiss what I just said. "The birds have been following all of us. Remember my scratched-up face from the encounter in front of the library? And my scalp's still sore from that night at your house."

I'm already shaking my head. "It's not like that. Not all the birds, just one." I clear my throat, rubbing my sweaty palms down my thighs. "It talks to me."

"Who talks to you?" she asks, looking at me suspiciously. "Don't tell me you can talk to spirits, too?"

"No," I say then turn a bit so I'm facing her. "The raven talks to me. Its voice is in my head all the time now. Telling me stuff, making me do stuff, asking me to do stuff." I stop because it's hard to say, harder to hear myself saying. I really want her to believe that a bird's trying to turn me evil. I guess it's just as high a probability as the fact that she can talk to and see ghosts.

"Wait a minute," she says, shaking her head. She's pulling her legs up so that it looks like she's kneeling on the bed. At the same time she's pulling the ends of that shirt she's wearing down. It's not working, I can still see a lot of her legs. My hands are still sweating.

"Are you saying that there's a raven following you? What's it telling you to do?"

I hesitate. This isn't as easy as I thought it was going to be, especially since I really want to touch her. I want to just sit here and hold her and kiss her and not think about all the dark stuff going on inside and around me.

"It knows about the power and things just happen, like all of a sudden I'm super strong. Stronger than I ever was before. And I'm so sick of these powers. I just want things to go back to the way they were." But I don't, not really. Before, I didn't know. Krystal and I thought my mom had left me because she wanted to.

"I don't understand. How can the raven talk to you? I guess that sounds strange coming from the one who sees and talks to spirits. But why you? Both me and Sasha have been attacked by the birds, but never any kind of verbal contact."

"I don't know why," I say and realize with a start that I'm still lying to her. Why? I should be able to trust her with all of the truth, not just bits and pieces. But I can't. What will she think of me if she knows I have evil in me? Will she still want to be my girlfriend?

"What about your powers? You said you're stronger. Is there anything else, like something new you can do?"

Did she want the long or short list?

"Along with the super strength is this super speed and you already knew I was starting to move things with my mind. Well, that's even magnified. I can move bigger things now, people and cars and stuff. And I just feel different, stronger, like indestructible."

"Wow," she says. "Well, that's good, I guess. That means all of us are coming into our full powers. We'll be able to fight whatever this is when we do."

"But how do you know what we're fighting, or if we're even fighting on the right side?"

"Fatima says—"

I don't even let her finish. "I don't care what Fatima says. She never really says anything."

Krystal's eyes get big as my voice rises and I sigh. "Sorry. I'm just getting tired of not really knowing." But I do, at least now I do. "I don't know how we, four teenagers with powers we've only really used for a few months, can fight this evil or why we were even chosen to do so."

"It doesn't matter," she says. "You have to have faith."

"What?"

"Faith is believing in things unseen, unheard and unknown. It's trusting that all things will work out for the good."

"Who told you that?"

"I learned it in church."

"It figures." I sigh again.

"What does that mean?"

She's offended, I can tell. That's not what I meant to do. "I'm just saying these are two different circumstances."

She shakes her head. "No. I don't think so. I think that we were given these powers for a reason, from some higher being. Why should we question that? Why can't we just take the powers and do with them as we were meant to?"

"Are you serious?" I look at her, asking because Sasha and I were the ones to convince Krystal that she needed to embrace her powers just a few months ago.

"I'm dead serious, Jake. I've had a lot of time to think about this. We all have a purpose to fulfill on this Earth, a destiny, I guess."

Destiny? Charon said something about fulfilling a destiny.

"I just wish we knew what we were supposed to do."

"Maybe we'll know when it's time for us to know." Krystal reaches out then, her fingers touching my cheek the way she does so often. In that second nothing else matters. I don't want to think about Charon or Styx or these powers or anything else. I just want Krystal.

I don't know if this is what she expected to happen when she touched me, but I scoot closer to her on the bed and lean my face into hers. She blinks at first then gives me a half smile which I take as permission. Next my lips are on hers, soft and warm is the kiss. Just the way I expected. But then something shifts inside of me and my arms are going around her body, pushing her back until I'm lying on top of her. I can feel her heart beating against my chest, or is that mine? I don't know, all I know is that I love the taste of her, the feel of her. She squirms beneath me and every nerve in my body goes on end. I can't breathe and then again I can, but the scent is all Krystal. She's seeping inside me, occupying every lonely space I've ever had, pouring into the heart that's been so empty for so long. I can't stop touching her, kissing her, needing her.

Her palms press against my shoulders and I almost don't notice, but then she tries to say something while my lips are still on hers. I pull back slightly, looking down into her eyes gone dark all of a sudden.

"We can't do this here," she whispers, and it dawns on me where we are and who is in this house with us.

Her parents, namely her stepfather, who is not the most friendly on an ordinary day when I knock on the front door to see Krystal. I can only imagine his response if he were to walk into her room right at this moment.

Let's just say I probably won't have to worry about Charon killing me for making the wrong decision. Mr. Bevens—her stepfather—will certainly take care of that.

I move off of her, lying beside her on the bed instead.

"Sorry," I say, trying to catch my breath.

"Don't apologize," she says. "I liked it."

"You did?"

In response she reaches between us and takes my hand, pulling it up to rest on her chest—well, over her heart—where I feel the speedy rhythm that matches my own.

I smile and so does she. We keep holding hands even though I have to take mine off her chest, otherwise I'm going to have a mild coronary right here in her bed.

We lie like this for a while, not saying anything, sort of just listening to each other breathe.

"I don't want anything to happen to you," I say finally because the thought has been going through my mind. After seeing Pace pulling her away, then not seeing her for a period of time, the fear of losing her has intensified.

"I don't want anything to happen to you either," she says.

"We'll both be careful then."

"Right," she says then leans over and kisses me on the cheek. "We'll be extra careful."

I lie there, with Krystal's head resting on my shoulder, her hand in mine, wondering what's going to happen when I go home. Is Dad hiding anything else? How about Pop Pop? And if they are, can I blame them? Look how much I'm hiding from Krystal. I didn't even tell her about my mom, and that's what I really came over here for. Because I was feeling so crappy about that whole situation I wanted someone to vent to. But when I saw her, all coherent thought was erased from my mind and we ended up the way we always seem to end up lately—quietly enjoying each other's company. Only this time I'm in her bed in the middle of the night. So not cool! The last thing I need is to get caught, so after a while and with as much reluctance as I've ever had in my life, I get up. Going to the window, Krystal stands in front of me.

"You're the best thing that's ever happened to me," I confess.

She looks shocked. "I really like you, too," she says with a shy smile.

Cupping her face in my hands I kiss her again, this time as if it was the first and possibly the last. I don't know where that thought comes from but it comes fast and lasts throughout the kiss. When I look at her again I feel like I've done what I came to do and that the rest will just be.

Krystal on the other hand, looks worried. She flings her arms around me in a wildly tight hug and says my name over and over again. I don't know what that means. Maybe it's some crazy girl thing. I don't know, but if I stay much longer the sun will be coming up. When she lets me go I don't look into her eyes, don't really trust what I might see there. I just turn and climb out the window, heading down the tree and back into the chilly night air.

I don't look back, but I don't have to. I know the raven's flying above my left shoulder.

sixteen

"Fatima says we need to keep an eye on him," Sasha's saying as I get ready to turn the corner.

I was late leaving gym because I couldn't find my clothes again. I know that's courtesy of Mateo and Pace. Immature pranks from seniors who think they're better than me. You'd think they'd give up by now, but I'm thinking that maybe they need a bigger reason to stay away from me.

Anyway, I figure I've missed all the buses, so it'll be walking for me. I've been doing much more of that lately. Walking from my house to Krystal's, from my house to Sasha's or down to the sub shop. Thing is, it's not bothering me at all. Like I've got endless amounts of energy now just waiting to be used.

But I know that's Sasha's voice with just the barest hint of accent and once I hear the name "Fatima" it's confirmed. But who are they talking about? And why wasn't I invited to this little meeting?

"I don't feel comfortable spying on him." This is Krystal talking. I'd know her sweet voice anywhere. My body tenses automatically. Apparently it knows her voice as well.

"But it's hunting him. It wants Jake. Did Fatima tell you why?"

Now that's Lindsey and she sounds like she's on the brink

of crying. And she just said my name, said something's hunting me. I should walk around the corner, break up their private little meeting, but I don't. I press my back to the wall and keep listening.

"She just said this is a crucial time for Jake and for us. That we all have to be very careful of the choices we make because those choices will affect the overall outcome of this battle," Sasha reports.

There's a sigh but I can't tell who it comes from.

"I'm beginning to feel like Jake here, I wish she'd just tell us everything and get it over with."

"One thing I know that Fatima didn't have to tell me is that there's a lot of unrest in the Majestic," Sasha offers.

"Who cares about what's going on there?" Lindsey says. "I'm worried about the here and now. What's happening with Jake is going to ultimately affect us. We've gotta do something."

Krystal says, "I'm with you, Linds. We've got to help Jake."

"We can't interfere," Sasha says.

It sounds like Sasha's throwing me to the wolves. That thought stings a bit because Sasha and I have known each other the longest. We've been close for years. Then again, that Fatima chick's got her so brainwashed lately.

"I won't stand by and watch him be hurt," Krystal says. "I don't care what Fatima or anybody else says. I won't do it."

"Neither will I," Lindsey says with conviction. "There's gotta be a way we can stop what's going on."

I think it's Sasha who huffs this time before saying, "We don't even know exactly what's going on. How do we stop it?"

Above, a flock of ravens swoops down to circle over their

heads. I thought for a minute they were going to give me away, but they didn't. They zoom right in on the girls, circling and squawking until the girls are running away screaming. When I figure they're long gone I push from the wall and take a few shaky steps. I can't believe they're talking about me like I'm some outsider. Like I'm not a part of the Mystyx anymore.

Hurt and confusion quickly turn into anger, which simmers and boils inside me as I walk home.

How dare they leave me out of a discussion that's clearly about me? And is Sasha now conferring with Fatima the witch woman about me? This is all bull! There's nothing wrong with me. I'm the same Jake I've always been, with a few enhancements.

That's it. The power.

They're jealous because I obviously have more power than they do or ever will. All the way home my thoughts churn. Walking onto the first step in front of my house something pecks me on the shoulder. Looking over, I'm not startled or surprised.

They will never understand. You are not like them.

I've heard this before, but this time, I believe him.

I'm in the house maybe fifteen minutes before there's a knock at the door. I hadn't even made it up to my room yet, since I'd stopped by the kitchen for a snack. Now, I'm heading down the hall to answer the door.

Dad steps out from the living room, ahead of me, and gets to the door first. It's not even five o'clock yet, what's he doing home?

"Good evening, officers. Can I help you?" Dad says, opening the front door.

I'm standing behind him but I can see the two cops standing in the doorway looking at and around him. Spikes shiver along my spine as I stand a little straighter, waiting for what they'll say.

"Can we come in?" one cop asks.

Dad nods and steps back to let them in. I fall a few steps behind him, still keeping my eye on the cops. Something tells me them being here is not a good thing.

The cops step inside and we all stand in the narrow hallway. "There have been some complaints about your son," the cop with the long mustache that looks like it should be spit on and curled at the ends says to my dad. The other one looks like Butthead from the *Beavis and Butthead* cartoon.

Dad doesn't even look at me. "What kind of complaints?"

"Vandalism for starters," Officer Mustache says, peering over Dad's shoulder to eye me. "Broken car windows, dismantled tires."

I stare right back, fingers clenching at my sides.

He continues, "Assault and stalking as well."

I was going to remain quiet, wait and see what they were accusing me of, then see how I was going to handle the situation. But now I can't help yelling, "That's a bunch of crap!"

Dad holds up his hand and my mouth clamps shut. "Who's initiating these complaints?" he asks.

"Doesn't matter," Butthead finally speaks up.

"I say it does. If somebody's accusing my boy of something I want to know who it is."

"Why? So you can take matters into your own hands?" Mustache says taking a step closer to Dad. "We're the only law in this town."

Dad doesn't back down.

Like father, like son, I guess.

"We have a right to know who's accusing us of breaking the law."

"There's no 'us,' just your boy back there. He's the trouble-maker, as we hear it. We also got a tip he might know about that missing busload of people from a couple months back. So we'd just like to take him in for some questioning."

"No," Dad says.

I'm still reeling over the fact that they think I know about the missing kids from the bus. How would I know about that?

"If he ain't guilty, then why can't we question him?" Butt-head asks, pulling his nightstick out of his holster.

My fingers are flexing at my sides. I don't think he can see them because Dad's in front of me, but man, I'd love to punch him just once.

"You come back with a warrant or a subpoena and we'll get our lawyer and think about talking to you. Until that time stay away from my boy," Dad told them in his taking-no-sh★★ voice.

He's pissed, I can feel the anger rolling off him like big fat waves slapping against my face. I'm not too happy either. Pace and Mateo must have run to the police whining about what's been going on between us. Funny how they start whining when I start fighting back. For as long as they've been picking on me, I've been taking it, not saying anything to anybody. Now, the big and bad seniors think they could just run to the cops and tell them everything. What a couple of punks!

Dad's slamming the door as the cops just walked through it. But that was just after Butthead turned to give me a warn-ing: "We'll be watching you."

Dad told him to get out. I wanted to tell him to go ahead,

watch all you want, you're not gonna like what you see. Because they're definitely not. Pace and Mateo aren't getting rid of me by reporting me to the cops. The next time I see them they're gonna wish they'd never decided to mess with me.

"What's going on?" Pop Pop says, coming down the hall.

He's using his walker today instead of the wheelchair. I saw it in the corner of his room this morning and figured it was going to be a day he didn't use it. He got in those moods sometimes, like he had to prove to us and himself that he could still get around without it. Today, however, he's not proving a thing. He's barely moving with this walker and leaning into it more than he should be. Come to think of it, he doesn't look well. His face is all drawn and he looks pasty. When he talks his chapped lips stick together. I go into the kitchen, ignoring his question, to get him a cup of water.

"It's those same boys, the ones that were bothering you in school. They're the ones who sent the cops over here, aren't they?"

Dad's right behind me, helping Pop Pop and his walker so we're all in the kitchen now. Everything he says is a question. He knows the answers but he's putting them out there anyway.

"Yeah, I guess."

"Did something else happen other than them messing with you at school?"

I'm holding the glass to Pop Pop's lips now, tilting it slowly so he can sip and it doesn't run down his chin and the front of his shirt.

"It's nothing, Dad. Don't worry about it."

"Don't worry when the police come knocking on my door

asking questions about my son? Come on, Jake, this is serious. If there's something I should know you need to tell me."

"There's nothing to tell. I'm dealing with the situation."

"What's the situation? If they're bullying you then we'll press charges."

"No!" I say adamantly. "I don't want the law involved, that'll just give them something else to hang over my head. I'll handle it on my own."

"You know what happened to those kids on the bus," Pop Pop starts talking. "He got to 'em. Needed their eyes so he could see everything that's going on around here."

"For Christ's sake, stop talking about that stupid damned power!" Dad yells.

"Everything revolves around that damned power, Harry. You've known that all along. When he took Cecelia he said he'd have Jake one way or another. You knew this day was coming. Denying it doesn't make it go away."

"I don't care what he wants, he's not getting my son!"

"And I'm not going into a state of denial, nor am I going to cower from these bullies. I'm sick of living in this box, feeling like I'm not good enough to breathe the same air as them. I'm just as good as they are. I'm more powerful!" I yell.

Saying the tension in this room is thick is an understatement. Each man, three different generations of Kramers, are about to throw their own little temper tantrum right about now. But it's way past time. We've walked around this house for years suppressing what we feel and what we think, it's a wonder we don't all have mental complexes.

"You are not to go near those boys, Jake," Dad says slowly, his thick eyebrows drawing together to create that nasty unibrow. He's really angry or really afraid, I can't tell which one.

But I'm really pissed off. I want Pace and Mateo to pay and it's all I can think about.

"They get to do whatever they want, say what they want and nobody cares. But when I stand up for myself the cops want to come looking for me. Well, they know where I am, come and get me!"

"Jake," Dad starts.

"It's the darkness. He's feeling it all over now," Pop Pop says quietly.

"Stop it!" I yell in his direction. "Just stop telling me half of what I need to know. If some evil mojo wants to come and get me then just let him try it!"

I'm so angry right now. A part of me wants nothing more than to tear something up. Then another part, like it's in the distance somewhere, is confused and wondering how I got to this place.

"Jakey boy," Pop Pop says in a softer voice.

"This isn't helping me. You aren't helping me by trying to hold me back and not being honest with me."

Both Dad and Pop Pop look totally stumped right now. They don't know what to say to me or how to take this outburst. I want to explain, but don't know that I can. So I storm out.

"They've got him, Harry. The dark's got Jakey by the throat," Pop Pop says, in a whisper.

seventeen

I didn't take the bus to school the next morning, walked the distance instead. All the while I thought of Krystal and what I wanted to say to her. The things I wanted to tell her. Fatima's trying to turn her against me. That thought kept me awake half the night. And it shows.

After my shower this morning I noticed the dark circles under my eyes, the hollowed look in my cheeks. Normally, as a guy, I'm not real into how my face looks. I mean, I don't want to look hideous but I'm not like primping all the time either. Still, this morning I cringed. I didn't look like me, which seemed just fine since I didn't really feel like me either.

The only familiar feeling was the ache in my chest when I thought of Krystal. When I replayed the conversation I over-heard yesterday, hearing the indecision in her voice as she tried to defend me, that caused more pain. If I could just explain everything to her, I'm sure she'd understand. I know I have this choice to make, but really there's no choice at all. I know which side I'm supposed to be on. I feel it every day.

I arrive at school before the buses and because I have break-fast and lunch vouchers I am allowed to go in before the first bell. The decision I finally made is a cowardly one, don't need anybody to tell me that. But it's what I've decided to do. Heading down the hall where my first-period class is I stop at locker number 107. I slip the folded piece of paper between the slits at the top and hope for the best.

I'm not hungry but my temples are throbbing, and since I didn't eat before I left the house I figure a carton of milk and a piece of fruit might not be such a bad idea. Heading to the cafeteria I see a couple of familiar faces, kids I knew and went to middle school with and don't normally associate with now. They all look at me, then turn to huddle in their little group. Just like at lunchtime, the cafeteria is divided into classes. Not classes as in junior, senior, etc. The kids I went to middle school with are going to the jock tables, as most of them play some sort of sport. There's a few at the goth table looking as if they may have actually stayed in that spot since yesterday at lunchtime. The table where the girls and I usually sit is empty, so I naturally migrate there.

From my position in the center of the room I see the differences but wonder at the hidden similarities. Take Judy Renquist, she's a junior this year, with fiery red hair and bold blue eyes. In middle school she had freckles and her hair was curlier instead of in the smooth waves it is now. She was teased and called Little Orphan Annie for years. Now, because her skin is considered alabaster, her hair a natural anomaly to the girls who live at the beauty salon, and she can hold a standing split on top of a pyramid longer than any of the other girls on the cheer squad, she's moved up in the ranks.

Barry Humplefeld used to stick his finger up his nose and suck that very same finger minutes later. That wasn't a memory he was likely to live through, so it's no real wonder he sits by himself by the juice machine.

I look at both of them now, neither of them speaks to me. I guess that goes back with the years as well. I don't know what my failing traits may have been in others' eyes. To my-self I can admit not being overly friendly to anybody, but is that really a reason to set me apart? I guess I sort of set myself apart. To an extent it seems that we can dictate how we will be perceived. If I'd wanted to be thought of as a jock in high school, maybe I shouldn't have quit the football team when I was in elementary. Maybe instead of steering clear of Pace and Mateo I should have tried to befriend them. Maybe they wouldn't be so hell-bent on punishing me every chance they got.

In the seconds I have that thought they're erased. Feeling sorry for myself used to come easily, now it leaves me with a sour taste in my mouth. Or is that the white milk I just downed in two gulps? Either way, I don't like it.

Mateo and Pace are jerks, there's no way around that fact. I don't know if it's the exact way they want to be perceived but it's the impression I got a long time ago. Now, I hate them. Yeah, I know hate's a strong word. Krystal would tell me I shouldn't hate anyone. Sasha would say they aren't worth my time, to let them live their sheltered lives and get on with my own. Lindsey doesn't really have an opinion about the class wars because she seems to get along with any and everyone.

That leaves me to fight this battle on my own.

Which actually is growing achingly familiar to me lately.

I watch her walk into the building feeling a bit like a stalker, since I'm standing between two sets of lockers at the far end of the hall. The temperature outside has fallen a bit and she's wearing a fitted jean jacket over a black shirt today. Her hair's all out, pulled back from her face so I can see the silver hoop earrings. At her wrist is the charm bracelet that I now know holds a Betty Boop charm, a silver cross and an *M* that doesn't really look like our birthmark but in Krystal's mind probably stands for the same thing. I like the way the bracelet jingles on her arm as she lifts her hand to remove the book-bag strap from her shoulder. Somebody says something to her, Carol Landon from my government class, and Krystal turns to her with a pretty smile. She's made a few more friends here at Settleman's since she's gotten used to the town. I think it's great that she's finding her place.

She opens her locker and I see my note fly out. Krystal looks shocked, then reaches to grab it before it slips to the floor. Out of nowhere Pace appears. Reaching out one long arm he grabs the note, holding it away from Krystal.

As she gives him a heated look I take a step out from between the lockers. She reaches for the note but Pace holds it up out of her grasp. He's laughing and drawing a lot of attention. Mateo isn't far behind and steps up to Krystal with his own nasty smirk. He snatches the note from Pace.

I'm already moving toward them, heat suffusing my face and the tips of my ears. They're going to do it. On instinct I know it and I should turn around and walk fast the other way. But I can't. It's too late now.

Mateo opens the note. I can hear his deep, cagey voice saying the words just as I push through the small crowd that's convened around them.

"You mean everything to me. I want to be totally honest with you about all that's going on," he says, changing his voice so that it sounds sing-songy.

"Stop it!" I say through teeth that are clenching so hard I think my jaw's gonna lock. "Give me the note, Mateo."

He looks at me, then down at the note again. A sick grin

spreads across his face and I know he's seen my signature at the bottom.

"Why don't you come over to my dirty shack tonight," Mateo continues. "It's not much but I have a bed and we can lay in it and have hot steamy sex!"

Everyone in the crowd laughs. Krystal looks like she's seen one of her spirit friends. Her eyes get bigger and her mouth gapes a bit as her gaze finds mine. I can't speak, embarrassment has a grip on my vocal cords all but straining them into noncompliance. In my mind I'm repeating over and over how sorry I am but I know nothing is coming out. She starts to shake her head, her eyes filling with tears.

"Tryin' to get laid, tracker?" Pace says, thrusting his pelvis.

"Fat chance!" somebody from the crowd yells.

"Even she doesn't want a tracker," Mateo says, ripping my note in half. "Find your own kind" are the last of his words as he tosses the pieces of paper in my face.

Embarrassment has opened the door to rage. I feel it roaring through my body, the strength I've been dying to unleash. It's like bolts of thunder, rolling until they reach their destination. I lunge for Mateo. But he's ready for me this time. He steps to the side and I fall flat on my face, sliding across the newly waxed tiled floor.

More laughter sounds behind me, fueling my anger. They're all laughing at me, making fun of me. Like always, I'm the butt of their jokes. I hate it! I hate them!

Hate! Hate! Hate!

Rolling over onto my back I look up at the ceiling at the fluorescent lighting. One by one they all burst, drenching the hallway in darkness. Now the laughter has turned to shrieks. Somebody's running, probably to get the principal, but it's too late for the school judicial system to handle this situation. Rising to my feet I stand in front of Mateo just as he throws a punch. I take it on the chin but don't move because I didn't feel a thing. With a startled look Mateo punches me again. This time I catch his fist, twist his wrist until he's bowing in front of me in pain.

Pace comes at me from the side, and with my other hand I reach out and grab him, lifting him off the ground. When I let him go he crashes through the remaining crowd of kids and into the lockers. I drag Mateo across the floor while he's screaming like a girl.

Inside I'm triumphant, for once in my life I've got the upper hand. And for all the kids around the world that are being mercilessly bullied either online or in person, afraid to go to school and in some cases scared enough to commit suicide, I toss Mateo and watch as he slams into the lockers so hard spit flies from his mouth.

More jocks charge me, and while I don't know them I fight them all off, feeling the strength growing, loving the ultimate feel of power, of supremacy.

Then I hear her.

"Jake." She says my name and it sounds so soft, so innocent. "Please stop this. You're scaring me."

It's Krystal and she's standing near her locker, tears streaming down her cheeks. I don't know how I could hear her speaking so softly over all the noise and chaos in the hallway, but I did. And the heat in my body simmers like it's been spritzed with water. The steam is still there but the burn isn't.

I can't look at her and feel glorified in my outrage. I can't hear her voice and feel proud that I've accomplished something. It's in her eyes, in the tears falling from her chin. The disappointment and the fear.

Before I can make another move I'm grabbed from behind and dragged away. I don't even fight it, when I obviously could have. I can fight them all and win, but Krystal's gaze stops me cold.

Later in the office when I'm questioned, when my Dad is once again called, I have nothing to say. No explanation and no recriminations. They're all against me, always have been. Nobody cares that Mateo and Pace have been hounding me since elementary school, nobody gives a damn how much they embarrassed me and Krystal today. So it's no use in trying to explain. They hang with the Richies so they're always right. Even when Dad tries to defend my actions and wants to place a formal complaint against Pace and Mateo, his words are discounted, the principal basically calling him a liar.

I want to yell in Principal Dumar's round, fat, sweaty face that he's the liar. He's the fake one taking up for those ignorant, ill-mannered rich kids so their parents will continue to throw money into the school projects. I want to wrap my fingers around his skin-layered neck and squeeze.

Now you see where you belong.

The voice sounds in my head and I welcome it. This time I grab hold of the words, embracing them, holding them close to me as the only truth I've ever really known.

Dad takes me home. He's silent and so am I. I'm expelled from school, my chances of getting into a good college all but dashed with one morning's events. Dad doesn't know what to say. I don't care anymore. Nothing I say is going to make a difference. Only my actions can speak for me now.

eighteen

ON MY ratty old desk my cell phone vibrates. Turning my head slightly so I can see it, I watch as the vibration moves it in little paces across the desk. The light from its screen is the only light in the room, its sound adding to the monotonous tick tock of my wall clock.

I've been in my room since this morning's fiasco at school. I don't know where Dad is. When we came into the house he went his way and I went mine. Neither of us wanted to talk. I think because we know there are no more words. Something's changed and we both know it. What we plan to do about it is anybody's guess.

But I've been lying here thinking of nothing really and then of everything. Mostly I'm thinking about my mom. She was a Mystyx and I never knew. She could manipulate light, that's what Pop Pop told me, when Dad wasn't around of course. That sounds like a good power to me, so how'd I end up a Vortex? I guess that's where Dad came in, his genes I mean. If Uncle William was a Vortex, then dark was already looming in the blood of the Kramer men. That would be a logical explanation for my mixture of good and evil.

The fact that my growing strength and courage are coming from evil and I'm enjoying it means I've made my choice. Yet in my mind I don't quite know if I'm an evil power. I guess my actions are speaking louder than words lately. Actions that I do not regret in the least bit.

See, this is what makes me think I can be different, that my dark powers can be used for good. I know that might seem like I'm trying to rationalize the choice I've made, but I don't see any reason why anything has to happen in totality.

Outside my window thunder roars so hard the house seems to shake. It sounds as if something ought to have broken in its midst. I jump a little, then settle back down quickly. It's just a thunderstorm, no big deal. But ten minutes later thunder roars through the sky once more. The windows shake and I almost fall off my bed. As soon as the rumbling is over there's deafening silence throughout my room. Even the tick tock of my clock has stopped. The electricity must have gone out, since it's a plug-in clock and we often lose electricity during a storm.

Never since I was a little kid have I been afraid of thunderstorms, but this is different. And I can't say that I'm really afraid, just sort of anxious and leery of what's going to happen. Because let's face it, I live in Lincoln, I'm a Vortex of supernatural powers, I've visited the Underworld and know that there's another realm where magical beings live—so I know that something's going to happen.

The storm sounds intense, rain batting against the window with fierce attitude. Wind is making some strange noise that's a cross between a wolf's baleful howl and an angry demon's tenuous moan. Why I break it down that way, I don't really know, but those are the sounds I hear. I should get up, go and check Pop Pop and Dad, make sure there are enough candles and flashlights at the ready. But I don't move. My mind wants to, but it neglects to send the message to my body. So I'm still as a board on this bed, eyes wide open as if something else is holding the lids wide so I don't miss anything. But all I see is nothing. I mean, nothing substantial, since it's dark. Shadowy outlines of the furniture and paraphernalia around my room are visible but nothing else.

Until…

My door creaks open slowly, just like in a horror movie. I can move my head to the side so that I'm watching who or whatever comes in. The shadow is slow-moving, but familiar.

"Pop Pop." I call his name but he doesn't answer, just stands in the doorway while the door opens in front of him.

To say it's eerie is an understatement, because at the exact moment the door opens all the way, tapping the wall behind it, a fierce streak of lightning sparks through the window illuminating Pop Pop's upright body. And by upright I mean he's not in his normal crouched-over position that he has when walking or even sitting because of his osteoporosis.

When I sit up, my feet hit the floor at the precise moment another bolt of lightning streaks through the room. I see him clearly then. "Pop Pop, what are you doing up? Is something wrong?"

He kind of cocks his head as he looks at me, as if I should already know the answer to that question. "Things are not what they seem. You should know that and keep it in mind. Your choice will affect them all."

"How?" I ask, anxious for him to tell me all he knows.

But Pop Pop doesn't speak. Instead he looks to the window like he's waiting for someone or something. I look to the window as well, standing up from my bed. Through the storm I see a light, small as a pebble at first but then growing and growing until I'm squinting my eyes to see.

The light shines brightly through my window, casting shadows on the far wall. Shadows that seem to come alive and are moving directly toward Pop Pop.

Before I can scream or react in any way, at my side I hear a sound like a gasp, and the moment I turn to him Pop Pop falls to the floor.

When I think of my life, it makes me angry.

When I think of Krystal possibly still pining away for Franklin, or even using me as a replacement, it pisses me off!

When I think of Pace and Mateo and their small-minded jerk attitudes, I want to break something.

I'm used to dealing with anger, it's been a part of me all my life. I've always been angry at something: Mom leaving, Dad working so much, Grandma dying, Pop Pop getting sick, kids at school, adults at school. You name it, I've been angry about it. Seems like second nature to me now.

Tonight, however, the anger's different, the feelings moving through me are foreign. And yet I'm embracing them.

The last hour has been eventful, more eventful than any other time of my life. Pop Pop collapsed, I yelled for Dad and we called for an ambulance. The siren was loud and broke through the noise of the storm as the vehicle raced down our street. All the while Pop Pop remained perfectly still. His eyes had closed and he looked as if he were sleeping while the paramedics worked on him. I think I knew it then.

At the hospital Dad went back into the room with him, only to come back out twenty minutes later with a somber look on his face. I didn't need him to say the words.

When I was finally allowed in to see him, or the shell that used to be my grandfather, I didn't know what to say or what to do. I'd never been that close to a dead body before. It didn't feel as weird as I'd once thought it would, possibly because it was my grandfather. And I didn't feel as sad as I thought I should, instead I was just pissed off. Because no matter what the doctors said or didn't do, I know this was no accident.

The truth was in the shadows, the ones that appeared on my bedroom wall just before Pop Pop collapsed. I could be angry with Charon, because somewhere deep inside I know the shadows had done his bidding. Or I could be angry with the world I was living in, the one that demanded our power be kept secret; the one that crapped on people like me and my family all the time; the one that gave kids like Mateo and Pace a free pass to do whatever they wanted.

Good and evil went beyond the gods and demons and the Majestic, they were here, in Lincoln, Connecticut, and throughout the world in so many shapes and forms. Wouldn't it be nice to have the upper hand, to have the power to do away with one or the other? The power that was right at my fingertips.

Now, standing in the hall at the hospital, so many thoughts and scenarios run through my mind, all of them beginning with the cruelty and unfairness of the world and ending with Pop Pop dying. Dead. Gone. Forever. My fingers clench and my temples throb. I feel nauseous and then I feel empowered, pushed to do something. I can't believe they couldn't do anything for him, couldn't save him. Isn't that what hospitals and doctors get paid for? The nurse said it was a massive heart attack. They have medication for that, or some such crap. Then why couldn't they bring him back? I knew the answer but it didn't stop the pain and fury now occupying every available crevice of my body. Pop Pop can't be gone. He shouldn't be gone. Because I still need him.

"Jake." Dad calls my name and the tone of his voice matches that stupid doctor's. I don't want to hear whatever he's getting ready to say. My head falls back against the wall and I close my eyes. Hopefully this will let him know I don't want to hear any more.

His hand grips my shoulder. "Let's go home, son. Nothing more we can do here."

Nothing more we can do. Nothing we can do. Nothing. Nothing.

The words play over and over in my head like a scratched CD. I want to scream. I want to cry. No, I want to fight.

Against life.

Against death.

Against any and everything that has ever caused me pain. I want to cause them pain right back.

"I'm not going," I say, pulling away from Dad's grasp. To say he looks shocked is an understatement. Then he sighs and drags a hand down his face.

"Look, Jake. We can talk about this more at home. I'm tired, it's raining buckets outside and I just lost my father, dammit!" The last statement comes out like a burst of air. I've never heard my father talk that loud or seen him look that serious. But it doesn't change my stance.

"I can't go back there," I say, the words sticking in my chest, lodging right beside the lump of sorrow.

Dad walks toward me, reaches out and hugs me close to him. His embrace is tight and at first I resist. After all, we're guys, we're not supposed to cry, and definitely not in public. But I don't think I can stop the tears from coming. I certainly can't stop the pain from ripping through my chest. I want him to be alive, to be breathing, to say something. I want my grandfather back.

My arms go around Dad and the sobs come full force. I don't care who sees or hears me, I don't care what happens from this moment on. Without Pop Pop none of it matters to me anymore.

Two days later we're standing in the cemetery, right next to Great-uncle William's grave. There's a six-foot hole there, with a coffin held up by what look like bungee cords, waiting to be lowered as soon as the last prayer is muttered.

Rev. Lawrence, from Krystal's church, is standing at the top side of the casket on this green felt material that I don't know if is meant to just look like grass or to help cover the still-damp ground. There are a couple rows of chairs behind me, but I don't feel like sitting. Neither does Dad. So we're both standing near the casket. It's the color of cement with a slight gloss to it. I have no idea why I'm noticing something as trivial as the color of my grandfather's casket. Especially when I'm feeling like my entire world has come to an end.

I know that sounds drastic. And yes, my dad, who has always been there for me and who has promised to stand by me no matter what, is right beside me. He's living and breathing and doing what he does best. Still, I feel so lost, so alone in this world now.

I am here, Jake. Always.

The voice comforts me. It probably shouldn't but it does.

The sky's still a dusty gray, has been for the last four days now. Some people from Dad's job showed up, and some older people who knew Pop Pop when he was of sound mind. I saw

Sasha, Lindsey and Krystal at the church, but I haven't spoken to any of them since I heard them talking about me that day after school. They've been calling me, but my cell phone is still on the desk in my room. Right where it was the night Pop Pop came in and collapsed.

I don't have anything to say to them. They're all against me for whatever reason. I did talk to Twan briefly as I was leaving the church, but he and his aunt just wanted to offer their condolences. Other than that my mouth has remained shut. Just like the rest of me.

I feel tingling in my biceps but I'm ignoring it. I don't want the power right now. This is Pop Pop's last day here on this Earth, at least for his body. I don't want it marred by thoughts of anything else.

The reverend is finished talking and people are walking away. Dad drops a hand on my shoulder. "You coming?"

I shake my head, unable to move and refusing to take my eyes off the casket.

"I'll wait in the car. Take your time," he says. I nod and wait for him to walk away.

Only when I think I'm alone do I take a deep breath and move a step closer to the casket.

"I just want you to know that I listened to everything you said, Pop Pop. I heard every word." Tears sting my eyes, but I try with all my might to hold them back.

"I'm not Great-uncle William. I will be better. I promise."

And just as I speak those words I move to touch the casket one last time. Its surface is piping hot, singeing my fingers. I pull my hand back, cursing as the sky crackles with lightning. The wind picks up and I turn around.

The rest of the townspeople walking to their cars probably

think we're about to get another thunderstorm. But I know better.

To my right about five tombstones over I see Krystal, Lindsey and Sasha standing, watching me. To my left I hear the flap of wings and know exactly what's coming.

"Run!" I try to warn them, but they don't move, just keep watching me.

As a swarm of ravens descends from the gray sky, I turn to face them. Holding my arms open wide I stop them where they are. "Get back!" I yell.

They stand still with their wings flapping, staring intently.

Then I hear something, like a ripping sound, then a crash. As I look behind me my eyeballs almost fall out of their sockets. The ground is breaking open, old caskets surging upward, opening to allow zombie-like corpses to roam free.

A putrid stench floats on the wind as a low howling begins to sound. I look back and the ravens have broken their stance. As the zombies approach me from one end, the ravens fall to the ground, rising again as the black silhouettes I'd seen before. I'm in the middle of a battle. Dead versus deader.

I look around frantically for some sort of weapon and instead see Krystal, head bowed, lips moving like she's chanting something. Sasha, who was once standing next to Krystal, is now right in front of me.

"You have to choose sides, Jake. It's us or them," she says.

"Don't tell me what to do," I yell at her because the howling is so loud I don't think if she was standing right next to me she could hear me.

"Fatima says—"

This time when I open my mouth there's a roar that shakes the ground we're standing on. I feel it then, the darkness. It's inside me now, from the tips of my toes to the pricks of hair at the base of my neck. I'm full of darkness and rage, and Sasha's in my way of total dominance.

"Don't say her name! Don't say anything to me!"

"Jake, he's using you. He'll kill you once he gets your power."

"No!"

"Yes, Jake," another female voice says, and I look over to see Fatima wearing all white, her red hair flying in rivulets behind her. "If he gets the Vortex the light will be swallowed and devoured. He will have all power, the world as you know it will be forever dark."

"Just like an eclipse," I say. "Styx creates the eclipse. She is the darkness and I am from her."

"Styx controls the eclipse, she gave you your power to help you fight when the time came. Charon will take all that you have. He will kill you like he did your great-uncle and your mother. And your grandfather."

There's a vibration in my head, like two sides of a war going at it no holds barred. Around me the zombies are attacking the black silhouettes. I guess I'm feeling their battle internally. I hear so many voices, feel so much anguish and so much strength I don't know what to do.

My head hurts, my skin burns as it feels like I'm literally splitting in two. The rage occupying one heated half of my body and the swirling coolness of the light holding up the other side.

"My uncle was a Vortex," I hear myself mumbling.

"In Charon's world there can only be one ruler. He believes it is his destiny to control all the worlds. He was collecting evil souls and demonic powers instead of delivering them to the

Underworld as was his job. Styx found out and cursed him. He vowed vengeance in whatever world he could get it. Here is where he's trying to gain control. You are the only defense on this plane, Styx cannot interfere here."

I almost sighed but for the chaos going on around me—finally I was getting some answers. But was it too late?

I hear screaming, like something's tearing the very soul from someone. A glance to my right shows me it's Lindsey as she falls to the ground holding her forehead and her stomach. The look on her face is one of anguish or uncontrolled pain. Sasha runs to her side just as I tear my gaze away.

"Listen to what I say, Jake. My message comes to you this time from not only Styx but from your mother."

"Mom?" I can't help but turn my attention to Fatima at this moment.

"She died so that you could live to choose. Her light could not cover you forever, but she tried. And when Charon came for her she sent you a Guardian to prepare you for this moment."

"Pop Pop is gone," I cry falling to my knees. "He's gone. Forever! And nobody cares!"

Somebody touches my shoulder. I think it's Fatima because the touch brings a coolness to that side of my body that was burning with heat.

"I care, Jake," a familiar voice says as another touch goes to my opposite shoulder.

The coolness spreads through my body as I look up to see Krystal. She's no longer chanting but standing beside me, just like Fatima.

"I care what you choose."

Lowering my head I feel the rage swirling in the pit of my

stomach. It's too late. What they're saying is too late. Fatima giving me answers is too late. I want to scream my outrage.

But when I look up again I see her.

"Your friend called. She said you needed me so I came. Again."

This is a voice I also know. One I've missed for the last ten years. As I look into her eyes I feel a clenching in my chest I've never felt before.

"Mom."

"Yes, baby," she whispers. "You've grown to be such a good boy, Jake. Good and strong. Now I need you to be strong enough to make the right choice. To fulfill your destiny."

Overhead it seems the sky is so angry it's breaking in two with bolts of lightning. The black silhouettes are everywhere, with even more ravens dropping from the sky. The heat is intense and pulls at me from every angle.

But as I look from my mother, to Krystal, to Fatima, the coolness overwhelms me. My mother's light coupled with Krystal's touch and Fatima's knowledge cocoon me. My legs tremble as I begin to stand. The tingling in my biceps stops, but I feel confident nonetheless.

Looking up toward the raging sky with my eyes wide open I mutter the words that may seal my fate. No matter, it is as my mother and my grandfather said before, it is my destiny.

"I am the light. I am a Mystyx!"

As if I'd pulled an invisible plug, everything stops. The ravens and black silhouettes disappear, zombies creep back into coffins that fall seamlessly into the ground. The sky is quiet, the wind still. When I look to my mother she is a fading sight but she's smiling and blowing me kisses. Like the six-year-old who boarded the bus as she watched from the curb her last day on Earth, I lift my hand, kissing my fingers then blowing toward her.

The ache in my chest is slightly lifted because I now know why she left me. Not of her choice but because it was time. I thought it wasn't Pop Pop's time, but looking over my shoulder I see that his casket too has descended into the ground just like the others in the cemetery. It was his time, as well.

And it was my time, to do what I had to do. To play my part in whatever this battle was. I stand strong and clasp the hand reaching out to mine, knowing that I did good. I did what I was supposed to do.

"Mine," Krystal says, looking up to me with that gorgeous smile.

Lifting her hand to my lips I kiss her fingers. "Mine."

"Yours," Fatima's voice interrupts just as Sasha and Lindsey come to stand near me and Krystal.

"The battle is yours, young Mystyx. Charon will not rest until he's either won or lost with finality."

"Does that mean he'll be back?" Sasha asks with a frown.

Krystal sighs. "He will be back, and the next time he's going to pull out all the stops. I've seen the battle, but I don't know how it ends."

"With pain," Lindsey says. "With lots and lots of pain."

nineteen

TWO WEEKS after Pop Pop's funeral Dad and I have an appointment with Principal Dumar and the two officers that came to my house. The minute I walk into the room I know things are not going to go my way.

I'm wearing slacks and a dress shirt. Thankfully I convinced Dad that a tie would be overkill. I hadn't worn a tie since the funeral and before that it was my middle-school graduation. I actually hadn't intended to put another one on until high-school graduation. Judging by the way Dumar's staring at me, that's probably not going to happen, not in Lincoln anyway.

"Why are they here?" Dad asks instantly, nodding toward the two cops.

Dad's wearing slacks, a dress shirt and a tie. He looks distinguished, important. Even if it's the same outfit he wore to the funeral.

"They have some questions," Dumar says.

Now he's the one who should be consulting a fashion magazine. His suit looks at least twenty years old and is this gray-and-yellow-looking tweed, I think you call it. It looks hot and itchy, and the puke-green shirt he's wearing with it is just awful. I'm not even going to address the tie or the scuffed shoes. Let's just say Dumar could use an extreme makeover.

"My son's not answering any police questions without a lawyer," Dad tells them.

Dumar holds up a hand. "Then I will be the only one asking questions."

"That's a lie," I say, which earns a scowl from Dumar and a warning glare from Dad.

"No. I don't see why they have to be here," Dad tells them.

I'm proud of him. Not that I haven't been in the past, but in these last couple of weeks Dad and I have grown a little closer, talking a little more. He's on my side. I know this now, not just because he's been saying it over and over, but because I can feel it. Especially now as we stand off against Dumar and the cops.

Dumar looks from the cops to Dad. "Look, I want to get to the bottom of what's going on just like you do, Mr. Kramer. There's been a formal complaint filed against your son by two boys at the school. I couldn't put the police out of this proceeding if I wanted to."

"Then anything said here is off the record. And afterward," Dad says, pointing to the cops, "I want to file an official complaint against those boys."

Officer Butthead scowls, while Officer Mustache just gives a curt nod.

"Fine," Dumar says and signals for the officers to take a seat. "This is Officer Colter," he says, returning to Mustache, "and this is Officer Butler."

The similarity in his real name and my made-up one for him is too funny.

"You think this is a laughing matter, kid?" Officer Butthead...I mean Butler, says.

"His name's Jake," Dad says.

When we're all finally seated Dumar opens a file. I guess it's a file on me but I've never seen it. "Mr. Kramer, since the first day of school there have been reports of incidents with your son and two other students."

"Say their names," Dad tells him. "If Jake has to sit here and be confronted by you and the cops you can say the other boys' names."

Dumar just nods. "The other students are Mateo Hunter and Pace Livingston. Now, these boys have stellar reputations in this school."

"Yeah, because they're jocks. Without them Settleman's wouldn't have a chance at the regionals," I add. Because we're the only high school in town, as far as school sports go, we compete directly with the schools in the next city instead of first competing in a local school district.

"I assure you that does not get them preferential treatment," Dumar argues.

I just give him a "yeah, right" stare.

"Now, I don't know what Jake's problem is with these boys but he continues to assault them."

Dad's shaking his head. "Mr. Dumar, that doesn't even sound right. Why would Jake confront not one but two boys, repeatedly? Don't you think there has to be something else going on here? Something else like bullying?"

"Sure," Butthead buts in. "Your son's bullying those boys."

"Right," I say. "I'm bullying two seniors, pounding on them every chance I get. That makes a lot of sense." Even though lately I have been getting the upper hand with Pace and Mateo, that's most likely why I'm sitting here now.

Officer Colter jumps up, leaning over the table toward me. "You need to learn to keep your mouth shut, boy."

Dad stands and leans over the table right back at Officer Colter. "And you're about to be reported to your chief for harassing my son."

Colter's face turns a girly shade of pink as he sits back in his chair. Dad might not have supernatural powers but he's sure fighting on my behalf.

"Tell him how long they've been bothering you, Jake," he says and my stomach churns.

I don't want to be a snitch. I just want to deal with Pace and Mateo on my own terms. Unfortunately, that got me kicked out of school, and after having a little time to think about it, I realize getting my education is a lot more important than keeping my mouth shut.

"It started in elementary. Just little stuff like throwing paper at me, calling me names. Just last year it escalated."

"Escalated how?" Dumar asks.

I shrug. "They'd post a few things in chat groups about me. Name-calling got worse and then they started pushing on me."

Dumar nods. "And this year you decided to push back?"

"Yeah," I say, slamming my hand on the table. "I'm sick of them thinking they're better than me, that I should bow down to them because they have more money than I do. They're jerks and I don't care what you say, if they bother me again, I'm fighting back. I'm not ignoring them anymore!"

Dad puts a hand on my shoulder and I shut up.

"It's all right, son. You've got a constitutional right to defend yourself. Just like the school has a right to do something about bullying. And if Mr. Dumar doesn't, I will."

Dumar drags a hand down his paunchy face. "Now, threats aren't necessary."

"It's not a threat, Mr. Dumar. I promise you if you and your staff don't do something about this situation I will go over your head. My son shouldn't have to come to school ready to use his fists to fight for respect. He shouldn't be faced with assault charges because some kids think they're better than him. And I'm not going to tolerate it."

Before Dumar can come up with a response to Dad's stellar argument there's a knock on the door and then it opens. I'm shocked to see Mr. Strickman coming in. He looks right at me and I feel like he's trying to tell me something.

"Excuse me, but I heard this meeting was taking place and I wanted to be sure I didn't miss it."

"Mr. Strickman, you've already filed your report on the incident that happened in your gym class. There's no need for you to be here," Dumar says quickly.

It's then that I notice Dumar's sweating. His wrinkly forehead is beaded with sweat and the thin strands of rusty orange hair are sticking to his pale skin.

Mr. Strickman holds up a hand to stop Dumar's words. "I wanted to make sure my report and my comments went on record here. Mr. Kramer, Jake shouldn't be the one expelled. Hunter and Livingston intentionally goaded and assaulted him. I've seen them do this on a few occasions, including the one in the hallway."

Strickman had been in the hallway that morning? I hadn't seen him. Then again, I wasn't really on the lookout for teachers that day.

"What, are you in cahoots with the trackers?" Officer Butthead asks.

Strickman sort of cocks his head, staring at Butthead like he can see right through him. "Are you in cahoots with them?"

And I don't know, but the way he says *them* has me wondering.

"No. No. Let's just calm down," Dumar says, huffing like he's run around the track a few times. With fumbling fat fingers he closes the folder he'd opened a few minutes ago. "Look, maybe I do have some of the facts wrong. But I'll get to the bottom of it. This meeting is over."

"No, it's not," Dad says. "My son needs to be reinstated. He shouldn't be put out of school for defending himself."

The cops look at Dumar but Dumar avoids their gaze like an addict steering clear of rehab. He looks at Dad instead. "He can come back tomorrow."

"And what about those boys?" Dad asks. "I want to know what's going to be done about them. Because if they keep harassing Jake I'll have them arrested."

Butthead makes a sound under his breath but Strickman adds, "And I'll back up any complaint Mr. Kramer makes with my own."

Now there are two people on my side, Dad and Strickman. I don't know how to react to this.

"I'll take care of it," Dumar says. "Don't worry. I'll handle it all."

Dad stands and I follow his lead. "Good. I expect you to. Come on, Jake."

As I follow Dad out of the room we're stopped in the hall by Strickman. He's wearing khaki pants and the school's white polo shirt. He looks like a college student instead of a teacher. He extends his hand to Dad and says, "I'm Dan Strickman. I've got Jake for gym last period."

Dad nods and shakes Strickman's hand. "Thanks for what you did in there. I just hope it helps."

Strickman smiles. "I think it will. See you in class tomorrow, Jake," he says to me.

He's got that look again, like he's saying something to me but not in words.

I just nod. "Yeah, sure."

Dad and I leave the school and instead of going home we head to Maggie's, where we share some burgers and conversation that has nothing to do with school or supernatural powers.

"How're you holding up?" Dad asks when he's almost finished his burger. "I know you've been through a lot and learned a lot these past few weeks."

I shrug, then think better of giving him a blasé answer. It's time I start trusting my dad a little more. After all, he's all the family I have now. "I guess I'm coping. I miss Pop Pop."

He nods. "I know. I do, too." Then Dad takes a couple fries into his mouth, chewing while he seems to be thinking of something else to say. "I miss your mom, too."

I can't believe he just said that. "How did she die?" I ask.

"All she ever wanted was to keep you safe until you grew up and she could explain everything to you. She wanted to teach you about the powers herself. But she didn't get the chance."

"I don't know how he found you, but she left me a note that morning after I'd gone to work that said things didn't look good but that you were the priority. That no matter what, Pop and I were to look out for you. Then she was gone."

His voice hitched then he cleared his throat. "I never even had a body to bury."

"Just like Uncle William." I sigh. "You think that's what happened with Pop Pop?"

"Pops was old and he was sick. But he also had knowledge

of this other world that I could never understand. There are some humans like that, you know. They know about that place and the ones that live there. Pop knew and he believed with all his heart. I think the one that wanted you knew that. I think he may have played a part in Pop's last moments, sort of giving him a supernatural push. But Pop's time on Earth was almost over anyway."

"That's why we had Pop Pop's body to bury?"

"Maybe. Or maybe it's just because he wasn't from that other world. Maybe they can't just take a human body. I don't know."

Then Dad reaches across the table, touching my arm.

"What I do know is that I love you, son. And I'm behind you in this mission you have. Although I'm not from that place, never doubt my commitment to you."

I nod, feeling closer to Dad than I ever have before. "I won't."

"Now," he says, picking up his burger and pausing before taking a bite. "Tell me about this girl you're seeing. Is she like you?"

I think about Krystal and all I can say is, "She's great."

Dad knows a lot about girls, some of which was a little weird hearing from him, but it's nice to be able to talk about everything with him, the good and the bad.

So even though this day started out a little shaky, it's ending kind of cool.

I wonder how long that will last.

"I'm getting my license in a couple of weeks," I say to Krystal as we're walking from the bus stop toward Sasha's house. We're meeting there again.

They invited me, so I guess that means things are back to normal. I'm still a little irritated that they were talking about me behind my back, but I guess if they thought I was in danger of becoming evil they didn't really have a choice.

"Cool," she says.

We're holding hands as we walk but she's looking the other way, kind of like she has something else on her mind.

"I've got some money saved. Dad says he'll match it and I can buy a car. Nothing fabulous, just something so I can stop supporting the public transportation system." I laugh a little, trying to get her attention.

"That should be nice," she says. But she's been strangely quiet today.

"Is there something wrong?"

She looks at me. "No."

I keep looking at her, knowing she's not telling me the truth.

"Well, yes. I mean, I've just been wondering how it felt. To like, be almost evil, how did it feel?"

Great, she's still thinking about that, too. I guess I should have expected it. I'd probably have more questions, too if I were her. "It feels weird and scary," I say honestly. "It's no fun not knowing who you are or what you're meant to be."

"Do you know now?"

A car drives by, adding a little noise to the otherwise quiet afternoon. I shrug. "I guess."

We walk a little farther and I ask a question that's been burning in my mind for days. "My mom said my friend called her, that day in the cemetery. Did you call her?"

For a second or so Krystal seems to hesitate, then she takes a deep breath and exhales. "Remember a couple months back when I called you to the cemetery?"

I nod.

"I told you there was something guiding me there, some spirit that needed me. For weeks I kept trying to figure out who the spirit was and what they needed. I didn't know until that moment when we were in the cemetery again. Watching you suffer with conflict, trying to decide what to do, was tearing me apart. And when I thought my own pain and fear would prevent me from convincing you to do the right thing, the answer came to me. I closed my eyes briefly and there she was. I'd never seen her before but I knew instantly who she was and how she could help."

Krystal, the medium and my girlfriend, had called my dead mother back from the afterlife to help save me. That was momentous, I knew. Still, I didn't really know how to digest it.

"Thanks," I say, knowing that it's inadequate.

Looking over at me, Krystal smiles and squeezes my hand. "Don't mention it," she says in a carefree voice.

But we both know what's happened between us is nothing to be carefree about.

Lindsey's coming up the other side of the sidewalk as we get closer. I look at her clothes first, because lately, with her I just don't know. She's wearing all white, sweatpants, T-shirt and baseball cap, with her long dark hair hanging through the opening in the back.

"I'm fine, Jake. How are you?" she asks looking right at me.

She's not smiling but she looks happier, like a huge burden has been lifted from her. I wonder if that burden was me.

"I'm good," I tell her even though I think she already knows.

Sasha opens the front door and yells. "Come on, you've got to hear this."

We move up the walkway and head into her house. Before we even take a seat, Sasha's talking.

"My dad's in Alaska. He called my mom last night, told her he was working on a new venture and he'd be there for a while. She's all excited thinking we'll be moving to Alaska soon, but yuck!" Sasha takes a much-needed breath, then continues. "Anyway, I talked to Fatima and she was strangely quiet when I mentioned Alaska. So I got to thinking, if Fatima's quiet and Dad's staying in Alaska, where is Mr. Bryant? I really think they're together working on that Project S. And if I'm right and they're working on it in Alaska, the question is why."

"The question is," Krystal says, putting her hands on Sasha's shoulders, "what have you been drinking, snorting or sniffing that's got you so pumped up? Take a seat and a deep breath, please." She pushes Sasha down onto the couch and sits beside her.

Lindsey flanks Sasha's other side. "It's a lot you're trying to get out, but we have time. Just take it slow."

Sasha's head full of curls is shaking. "No, we don't have a lot of time. It's dark there, don't you see. All the time it's dark, that's why they're there and I'll bet the demon that was haunting Jake, that Charon character, he's there, too."

"Wait a minute, what are you talking about? Why would Charon be in Alaska?" I ask.

Sasha sighs. "I just told you, it's dark there."

"And?" Krystal and I ask at the same time.

"They can hide in plain sight if it's dark. Whatever their plan of attack is now, it happens there, in the dark."

We're all quiet, not real sure we understand what she's saying.

Then Lindsey starts to nod her head. "Barrow, Alaska. On November eighteenth the sun goes down and doesn't rise again until January twenty-fourth."

I wonder why she knows this but then remember she's like a walking encyclopedia, keeping facts in her head like she's one day going to get paid to do so—or, quite possibly, need them to save the world.

"Wait a minute," Krystal says. "So he's gone. The Darkness is no longer in Lincoln?"

I shake my head, because I, unlike the rest of them, can feel the answer. Don't ask me how, I just do. Almost like déjà vu, I just know. "It's still here. He has to keep an eye on us. We're still the ones to stop him, no matter where he goes, so he has to watch us."

"Why us?" Krystal asks.

"It's our time," I say. "On Earth, at this time, it is for us to stop the evil that threatens to tilt the balance in all worlds."

"How do you know that?" Sasha asks.

"Because he is a Vortex," a female voice answers.

All eyes turn to the window where the orb of light comes through. It was a silent entrance, one that none of us were aware of until she'd spoken. But now we see her in all her otherworldly glory.

Fatima.

"His life is a mirror of the Vortex before him," she says coming closer to us.

"Uncle William," I whisper.

twenty

"William Kramer was a Vortex who has left this Earth, but you, Jake, are still connected to him. By blood and by power," Fatima says.

"So will he, like, always know what's going to happen before it happens now?" says Lindsey, who is sitting on the arm of the couch now because she's gotten up, walked around, then sat back down about three times since Fatima's appearance. I don't know what her problem is, maybe both she and Sasha drank one of those energy drinks, or two or three.

Fatima shakes her head, flaming red hair moving along her shoulders, a huge contrast to her pale skin and white dress.

"William may not have known everything before it happened. But Jake will have some advantage now because William has been through a battle of his own."

"He fought for the light, didn't he?" I ask, because thinking that my great-uncle could turn evil has been hard for me to swallow. I wish Pop Pop were still here so I could tell him that Uncle William didn't choose to go bad.

"William did what he thought was best. Unfortunately, he didn't have friends with him as you do, Jake. He didn't know much about the magical world. So when they came for him he couldn't handle it."

"But he wasn't evil. He didn't choose evil," I insist. I need to believe this, to believe that someone who shared my blood couldn't choose to end life instead of preserve it.

Fatima smiled. This was the first time I really saw a reaction in her. Well, at the cemetery she seemed pretty adamant about what I needed to do, but still she'd reminded me of some kind of robot just spouting words. This time, though, her smile looks genuine.

"He was not evil and therefore Charon could not use him. But finding out cost William his life."

I sink back onto the chair because that's all I wanted to hear. From her spot on the chair across from me Krystal smiles. I know she probably wanted to hear that, too. The fact that I might have been evil still freaked us both out.

"So what now?" Sasha asks. "We go to Alaska to fight him?"

"Charon is clever," Fatima speaks. "He was a high-level liege to the Underworld when Styx cursed him."

"Why did she curse him?" Lindsey asks. "I mean, why not just kill him, drown him in that sick water of her river. Why leave him alive to wreak this kind of havoc on the worlds to come afterward?"

I was with Lindsey. If Charon was so bad and pissed Styx off so much, she should have just toasted his demonic butt and been done with it. If she had we wouldn't be here right now.

"Because she's not inherently evil. Styx was given the river to guard, turned into a goddess by Zeus after she helped him win the battle against the Titans." Fatima moves closer so that she's now standing in the middle of the room, her feet not even touching the expensive rug on the floor. We're all sitting around her like pets thirsty for knowledge and possibly a pat on the head for a job well done. Silly, but true.

"Charon wanted more power. He believes it is his destiny to rule a world blanketed in darkness. He has been trying to go against Styx's curse forever."

"And he'll keep on, just like the Devil keeps fighting against God and his angels," Krystal adds.

Of course she'd think along those lines, and while none of us add any credence to what she's said, I can't help but think about the similarities as well.

"In every world there are chosen ones to thwart his efforts. As Jake said, in this world at this time, it is you, the Mystyx."

"But how do we fight him?" Sasha asks.

"Keep him from gaining power. You've done that when you pushed the darkness from that teacher it possessed," she says looking at Krystal. "When you stood up to his anger and saved Krystal from losing the portals of her soul in that forest."

I remembered both those times, at the school with Mr. Lyle and in the forest with…Franklin.

"And just a while ago when the Vortex chose to stand with the light."

All eyes fell on me.

"But he is not finished," Fatima adds. "He will keep trying."

"Then whatever we do is for nothing. Why even keep trying?" Lindsey crosses her arms over her chest.

"Because at the designated time, in the designated place, Styx will be there. She will lend her power to yours and Charon will be banished for all remaining times."

Okay, is it just me or did that just sound like a roundabout answer for she's still not telling us what we have to do to get rid of this demon?

And of course, Fatima picks that exact moment to have her

body sucked into a tiny white light that floats back across the room and through the window that she'd first appeared in.

"Crap!" I stand, yelling. "Still with the half answers. I thought we were finished with this secretive stuff."

"She answered us this time, Jake," Krystal says softly. "We're fighting an ancient battle, the one between good and evil. A battle that may never end, but still needs to be fought."

"And," I say, moving my hand like I want her to continue. "How does that help us know what to do to fight it?"

"Maybe we just figure it out as we go along," Sasha adds.

"Yeah," Lindsey says nodding. "Maybe we'll just know what to do when it's time to do it."

I fall back into the chair not looking at any of them. "That idea sucks."

twenty-one

sasha's driving way too fast. She's taking corners like she's behind the wheel of a police cruiser in hot pursuit instead of the sports car her father gave Mouse to chauffer her in.

"Where'd you say Mouse was again?" Krystal asks, holding on to the door handle to keep from sliding across the backseat.

I'm doing the same and shaking my head at the same time. I don't know which instructor Sasha had during driver's ed, but they should be fired.

From the front seat Sasha waves her hand. "I don't know where that big oaf is. He's been disappearing a lot lately. I'm half tempted to follow him to see what secrets he's hiding because I know he's hiding something. But instead I figured now was our chance to go out without him hovering over us."

"So where are we going, and when did you say you got your license?" I ask.

In the front passenger seat Lindsey sighs. "She didn't get it. Jumped the curb then yelled at the testing agent. He told Mouse to take her home and leave her there."

"Thanks a lot, Miss 411," Sasha says with a frown. "And for your information, I was doing just fine until I saw something that shouldn't have been and got all distracted."

"What'd you see?" Krystal asks.

Sasha shrugs. "Nothing important, I guess. I mean, since my power changed I've been seeing a lot of magicals down here walking around like they belong. But sometimes it still rattles me."

I'm praying my seat belt works as we keep moving at this high rate of speed. "So you saw a magical at the DMV?"

"It was the testing agent. He had fangs the size of Dracula's, so every time he said something to me I freaked. And the last time he touched my arm I wanted to jump right out of the car. Instead I turned the wheel too soon and jumped the curb."

"They fail you for that, you know," Lindsey says, trying to hold back her grin.

"Yeah, no kidding." Sasha smirks.

"So why are you driving without a license?"

"Dang, Krystal, you're so uptight. We're not in some big city, who cares if I don't have a license in Lincoln? There's hardly ever anyone on the road to hit anyway."

And the moment she says that something darts out of the woods in front of the car. Sasha swerves to keep from hitting whatever it was. All the girls scream and shriek and I wish to any higher being that Twan had come with us instead of taking his aunt to the doctor. When the car finally comes to a stop I feel like I've got whiplash.

"We're here!" Sasha yells and jumps out of the car.

Giving Krystal a weary look I unsnap both our seat belts and we get out.

Lindsey's already out of the car but she's standing perfectly still. "Feels funny here."

"Funny like we almost hit a deer and got ourselves killed,"

I say in a voice I know is drab and borderline angry, which I'm still trying to work on.

"No," Lindsey whispers and walks ahead of us. "Funny, like we probably shouldn't be here."

Sasha's already deeper into the woods and Lindsey's following her. I start to walk behind them but notice that Krystal isn't following. She's still standing by the car looking as if she might actually cry. Going back, I stand in front of her and take both her hands in mine.

"What's the matter?"

She takes a deep breath then sighs it out. "Memories" is all she manages to say.

I nod. Remembering her in Franklin's clutches deep in the forest that day doesn't sit well with me either. But Sasha has a reason for being here. We owe it to her to find out what that reason is.

"It's okay. I'll stay right by your side."

With quivering lips she smiles. "You will?"

"I will. You're mine, remember. I'm not about to let you go now." Leaning forward, I brush my lips over hers and resist the persistent urge to press further. "Let's go."

With her fingers entwined in mine we start into the woods to try and find Lindsey and Sasha. It's not hard, since they're both glowing like lightning bugs. That's no exaggeration. Sasha's pink light and Lindsey's purple light from their birthmarks illuminate the area where they stand. Once Krystal and I make it into the clearing, our lights burn bright as well.

"Where are we?" I ask, looking around. It looks like any ordinary forest area with a clearing full of brush and downed trees. Only it's not quite the same as anywhere I've ever been.

"This is where they found that bus," Sasha says. "I read

about it in the paper, the exact location, I mean. After those bodies were found we were all wondering about the connection to the Darkness. I figured it was past time to come and check it out."

I keep looking around, trying to see beyond the tall trees because it feels like something's out there. "Yeah, the cops think I'm involved somehow so I guess it'll help if I can give them some real information as to what happened."

"You?" Krystal asks from beside me. "Why do they think you're involved?"

I shrug. "I think Pace and Mateo may have put that thought in their heads. I don't know. But one day they came by my house talking about it, wanting to ask me about it, but Dad said no."

"Oh, my God, Jake. Why didn't you tell us this before?" Sasha asks.

"Didn't think it was important."

"If the cops are looking at you for a crime like this I'd say that's important," Sasha adds. She's getting all fired up, her eyes glaring at me.

"They don't know how he's connected, they were just fishing for information," Lindsey says. "Right, Jake?"

I nod because I still can't stand that she can get inside my head. "Yeah."

"We absolutely cannot keep secrets from each other," Sasha says with hands on her hips. "Whatever information we come across we have to share it when it happens. You never know what might be crucial."

"Okay, Sasha. Don't get all wacked out about it. I didn't tell you because I was going through some things at the time. You know, being seduced by evil, harassed by bullies, then losing my grandfather, that kind of takes a lot out of a person. You can see how easy it would be to forget small details like a visit from the police, right?"

At my side Krystal rubs my arm. Lindsey looks apologetic and Sasha, in a way that was only befitting of her, comes stomping right up in front of me and punches me in the shoulder.

"Don't you dare make me feel stupid for yelling at you, Jake Kramer. I can be mad if I want to." But her eyes are watering.

"Cut it out. We're cool. And you're right, we shouldn't have any more secrets." If she cried I wasn't going to be able to stand it. Me plus girls plus tears did not mix well at all.

"Okay, no more secrets," Lindsey says, putting an arm around Sasha. "Now show us what you wanted us to see."

After a few sniffles Sasha takes a deep breath. "I don't really know. I just got this feeling last night that we should come out here and have a look around. I mean, that bus disappearing and those two bodies showing up with their eyes missing is no coincidence. The police don't seem to have any clues, but then they're not looking with supernatural eyes."

"And you think the bus disappearance was supernatural?" Krystal asks.

"Yeah. Don't you?" was Sasha's reply.

"I guess you're right. But where's the group leader and the rest of the kids from the bus? Shouldn't they have been found by now?"

Krystal raised a good question, one I'd been thinking myself. "Unless someone's not ready for us to find them."

I move away from the center of the clearing, kicking leaves and branches out of the way as I go. Something's here. I can feel it. There's an energy in this area, like a pool of power. And it's feeding something, or someone.

Me, I hadn't felt the power surges since that night in the cemetery. My biceps hadn't twitched, but they hadn't gone down either. I tried to do that running and jumping thing like I did out and back into the window before, but it didn't work. I guess these powers were part of the evil growing within me and once I denounced the darkness, the extra power went with it. I can still move stuff with my mind and I bet if I punch Mateo I'd break his jaw as well as send him flying a few feet. But those extras, along with my red-eyed raven, are gone. And I can't really say I miss them.

But there's power here and it's doing something. My gaze falls on the trees again and this time I see inscriptions in the trunk. Moving closer, I lean forward to get a closer look. It's symbols or something, just like the ones on that scroll I found in the yard that day. I'd put that scroll in my bottom drawer and hadn't thought about it since then. Until now.

"What is that?" Krystal asks from behind me.

Lindsey's suddenly at my other side. "It's Greek letters," she says.

"Can you read it?" I ask, because I wouldn't be surprised if she could.

She shakes her head. "No. Not without my notebook, and that's at home. I know this is Alpha and this is Omega," she says, pointing to two different symbols. "The Beginning and the End."

"The Beginning and the End," I say softly, remembering that I'd heard that before. "They were the Beginning and we are the End."

"What are you talking about?" Sasha asks.

"Charon said it to me one time, that they, Styx and the gods and goddesses of her time, were the beginning. We, the Mystyx, are the end."

"The battle ends with us," Krystal adds. "I don't believe that. Good and evil have been fighting for a long time. To think we have the power to end that once and for all just doesn't sound right. Besides, as long as there's free will evil is bound to find its way back."

"She's right," Sasha says. "But maybe we can put an end to Charon's threat. Maybe that's our part and the rest is left for the next group of Mystyx, whomever they might be."

Lindsey's about to say something, but Krystal's cell phone rings. She answers and then hangs up. "There's trouble coming. My mom says the mayor's issued an evacuation of all homes. There's a category-five hurricane heading our way. We need to get back."

"A hurricane in Lincoln, Connecticut, in November?" Lindsey asks as we're walking back to the car.

Sasha gets to the driver's side door, then stops to look at us. "Just like sixteen years ago when we were all conceived. Remember, Pop Pop told us about it?"

I did remember. With a heated pain in my chest I remember my grandfather and all his stories. But as we ride back into town, the sky darkening above, I think about that night. Not that I can remember it, but I just imagine what it would have been like.

All the roads would have been closed, businesses shut down, everyone warned to stay in their houses until the storm passed. My parents would have been living alone back then, passing the time as many other shut-in couples did. And I was conceived. On a stormy night filled with excess energy that birthed these powers.

I wondered what would be birthed as a result of this storm.

twenty-two

Dad's already boarding up windows by the time I get home. Falling into step right beside him I pick up one of the boards and stand by as he heads to the next window in the living room.

"Hasn't been an ordered evacuation in Lincoln since before you were born," he says, taking the board from me and putting it up to cover the bottom half of the window.

I reach down into his toolbox and grab a couple of nails, handing him one at a time. "Really? You think the storm's going to be that bad?"

He cocks his head to the side, looking at me for a minute. Then he resumes his task banging the nail into place. "Let's see, you pissed off a powerful demon by choosing to stay on the good side. Pop, who was your Guardian, is now gone and your mother, who's been gone for ten years, is suddenly showing herself to you. I'd say this storm is going to be worse than anything we've ever seen."

And with that assessment Dad just proves my worst fear. On the drive back we were all quiet, most likely trying to convince ourselves that this storm evacuation had nothing to do with us or what was going on in the Majestic. Apparently our silence wasn't enough to make it so.

"I haven't heard him since that day at the cemetery," I say.

"He's pissed off."

I nod and get another board for the last window. "Yeah, I guess. I still don't know how to fight him."

"That makes two of us," Dad says, and scoops up the tool-box. "Let's move the photos and stuff upstairs and get them wrapped in plastic and put into trunks before we head over to the library."

"Right," I say, following him.

Lincoln's library is the biggest facility we have, except for the mall, but that has way too much glass to be considered a good place of refuge. We'd be like sitting ducks by the time the winds hit. I doubt the entire town's going to fit into the library, but the entire town probably won't evacuate. There's always those that think they can ride it out. Pop Pop would have been one of them. He wouldn't have wanted to leave his house just because somebody else told him so. He was like that, a man who lived by his beliefs. And so was Dad. I guess this is the first time I really see the differences in them and the similarities. Dad was doing what he thought was best, all the while acknowledging that this could be really bad.

Moving throughout the house, we finished packing up what we could. Dad emptied the little safe where he kept all his extra cash; he didn't really trust the banks. Running back upstairs I retrieved my jar of savings, stuffing it into my back-pack. It wasn't like we wouldn't be coming back home. Then again, we didn't know that.

Half an hour later we were pulling our car into the back parking lot of the library. It was crowded but everything seemed to be going along in an orderly fashion. The dozen or so cops and firefighters standing in the streets directing traf-fic and groups of people were probably the cause of that. In all my life I'd never seen Lincoln look so busy, so congested. For a minute you'd think we were a big city, but as we approached the entrance to the library we were forced to think again.

This was no state-of-the-art building. It was old redbrick, three stories plus the basement, about three small-town blocks long with no elevators and old-as-dirt vending machines that never worked. The selection of books was good, suited our public school system well, I guess. I rarely found what I needed here now, opting to use the Internet more and more.

"Hey, man." I turn to see Twan standing behind me.

"What's up?" I nod in his direction. He's standing with a woman who has two shopping bags in her hand. Twan has a backpack like me and two bags in his hands, as well.

"Auntie packed everything we couldn't nail down," he says with his usual chuckle.

I grin back because Dad and I tried to do the same with what we felt was valuable. Funny how we each only had one bag.

"This line's moving way slow. Hope the storm waits for everyone to get inside," Twan says.

"The good Lord waits for no one," the woman who I assumed was Twan's aunt said. She had a stern but caring-looking face, and while her eyes looked deadly serious as she spoke, something about her stance made me feel like I could like her.

"That's the truth," Dad says to her with a nod of his head.

I'm like, what? I've never heard Dad speak of a Lord being good or bad. Then again, we've never been standing in line to get into a shelter before a super-wicked hurricane hits us either.

After about a half hour of stop-and-go movement we finally make it through the heavy doors of the library. They're glass, too, I note, but they're boarded by some heavy tarnished bronze that'll probably withstand the winds and then some.

Once inside, Twan and I immediately thought of where would be the best location for us to set up. People were choosing their corners first, then heading to the middle of the main floor to get things like blankets and pillows and water bottles.

"Third floor's gonna be the safest. It's the highest ground we can get to," Dad says.

Twan's aunt, who told me about fifteen minutes ago to call her Aunt Pearl, agreed. "Well, let's get to the stairwell. You boys can come back down and get our supplies."

Following the adults, I watch my dad take one of Aunt Pearl's bags and help her with the two landings of steps. The third floor has the only conference room in the library, which holds about fifty people and is currently filled to capacity. We keep moving down the hall past the international book section. The bathrooms are to one side, but we walk through another doorway and we're in the tax section. I guess just as in real life everybody tends to avoid anything to do with taxes if they can. This corner is just about empty. Dad and Aunt Pearl are already heading to a corner away from the windows, pushing tables to the side as they go. Pulling one of the chairs along with him as he walks, Dad props it against the wall and tells Aunt Pearl to sit. He then turns to me and Twan and nods for us to go get provisions.

"Your dad seems pretty cool," Twan says as we move down the stairs trying to avoid bumping into other people as we go.

"Yeah, so does your aunt."

"Hey, you think the girls are coming? I tried to call Sasha on her cell but didn't get an answer."

"When I left them earlier, I know Krystal and her parents were planning on coming. I don't know about Sasha and Lindsey. Sasha's house is pretty big, they might be safe enough there."

"Yeah, but who's going to board it up and make them safe? Her dad's MIA remember?"

I remembered and it bothered me, but probably not as much as it was looking like it bothered Twan.

"I think they'll probably come," I say more to comfort him than because I really believe it.

On the main floor we stand in another line, and who should I see across the room just entering the building but Mateo Hunter, his mother and his two sisters. The tension must have showed on my face because Twan claps me on the shoulder.

"Don't worry about him, man. I got your back."

I nod my thanks but get the feeling that I won't need Twan's protection. Mateo doesn't look my way, but he looks plenty angry. I don't know if it's because he's here or for some other reason, and after about fifteen seconds I decide not to care either way. As long as he steers clear of me I'll stay away from him. That's what Principal Dumar had advised anyway. I heard Pace and Mateo both got some kind of probation from the school board and the cops. If either of them got into trouble during the rest of the school year they'd be instantly expelled, a huge blemish to the Ivy League college hopefuls. Dad wasn't totally pleased with the judgment, and while I didn't think it was a hundred percent fair I just didn't want them in my face anymore.

We were on our way back up the stairs when I saw Krystal

and her parents. Walking right behind them was Sasha and her mother. Twan's walking away before I can even say a word. Of course I follow him until we catch up with the girls.

"We've got a space up on the third floor. Get your stuff and head on up there. We're in the tax section," Twan tells Sasha.

"You don't even like to pay a tip," she says, smiling at him. "What are you doing in the tax section?"

"Jake was leading the way," he says.

"Hi, Mr. and Mrs. Bevens," I say to Krystal's parents. Her mom's looking at me with a small smile while Mr. Bevens gives me that barely tolerant look. Something's just not right about this man, and it's not just because I hear Krystal complain about him all the time. This is an entirely different feeling that I get whenever I'm around him. Maybe it's because he's another man in Krystal's life or some other such male rivalry thing. I don't know, but her mother speaks and a few minutes later I watch all of them entering the tax section where we'll be spending an unspecified amount of time together.

"Where's Mouse?" I ask Sasha when we put some distance between us and the adults, who seemed to be making cordial conversation.

"He dropped us off. I don't know where he's going or if he's coming back," she says.

"That dude is some kind of weird," Twan says, sitting on the floor beside the chair where Sasha sat.

"Anybody hear from Lindsey?" Krystal asks, pulling up a chair for herself.

"Nope," I say and look toward the door like I expect her to walk through at any second.

Instead, through the windows we hear the first whistles of wind start to pick up.

"Hope she gets here soon," Sasha says and reaches for Twan's hand.

I scoot my chair closer to Krystal's as we prepare for whatever's coming our way.

"Yeah, me, too," she says in a soft voice.

I hope the storm gets here soon. The sooner it hits the sooner it'll be over.

I hope.

It didn't take long for us to become bored out of our minds. About one hour and ten minutes to be precise, right about the time all visibility through the windows was shot. Electricity had blinked out about twenty minutes ago, but flashlights and small battery-operated camping lanterns had been given out when we picked up the blankets and pillows.

So we all had a flashlight and were walking around the library, well, through the halls and stairways. We hadn't planned on going into any of the areas where there were actual books because they were mainly occupied by people. But Sasha had a suggestion that had us heading back downstairs to the first floor.

"We should get as much information on this Charon character as we can. Since he's who we're fighting against, we should know all his strengths and weaknesses."

"And we'll find that out how?" Twan asked. Clearly Sasha hadn't told her boyfriend everything that had been going on with us, including all the new developments. Twan hadn't mentioned my issues at the funeral even though I'm sure Sasha probably told him that, too.

"Well, duh, we're in a library," she says.

Lindsey, who just appeared, like she often does, about a half hour ago, pulls her hair up into one of those rubber-band thingies so it's sitting on top of her head like a nest now. "We're in a library with no lights, how do you expect us to find the appropriate books, let alone read them?"

Sasha sighs, her frustration level clearly at its peak. "We've got these, don't we?" she asks, waving her flashlight around so that the stream of light wiggles across the walls of the hallway as we walk.

"I can think of better things to do in the middle of a hurricane than reading some books about a demon guy," Twan says. I can't see exactly what he's doing but I can hear his lips making a smacking sound just before hearing another exasperated sigh from Sasha.

"We can do that later," Sasha says.

Twan groans, and I sort of sympathize with the guy. I mean, I know I'd certainly rather be sitting in a dark corner with Krystal right next to me than walking through these dark halls while a storm rages outside.

I laugh and beside me Krystal clears her throat. "I guess we could look him up, see what history says about him."

"History's going to say what we already know, he's evil," Lindsey says dryly. "Besides, I've been thinking, if Charon has moved on to Alaska, how is this battle still ours? Wouldn't there be another group of Mystyx there to fight him off?"

"Maybe," I answer. "Maybe not."

Lindsey keeps going as we hit the last landing of stairs. She stops in front of the doorway with the exit sign above it. "So we have a global responsibility now?"

"I don't think it works in sections. It's sort of assigned to us in this time," I say, giving the best answer I have. Of course, I don't know if this is the correct answer, just adding my thoughts I guess.

A loud rumble sounds and the walls around us shake.

"Wind's picking up," Twan says.

"That new weather guy said it would be a category-five hurricane," Sasha adds.

Twan sounds like he's smirking when he responds, "That guy doesn't look too confident in his own predictions."

"It's going to be bad," I say.

Krystal touches my arm. "How do you know?"

"I just feel it. Danger, catastrophe, pain. Destruction is in Charon's heart and he is the heart of every storm. He told me that."

"So he can do all this, and he still wants more power?" Twan asks.

I'm really amazed at how well Twan's taking all this supernatural talk. I mean, when I first told him there was a moment of disbelief, but after Sasha walked in and he looked at her, he simply accepted everything we said. That must be one amazing connection those two have.

"Greed," Lindsey says on a sigh. "Isn't that the main issue with all evil beings?"

"You're right," Krystal says.

"And we didn't even need to find a book to tell us that."

Twan gains another exasperated sigh from Sasha and a chuckle from me and Krystal. Lindsey's standing there but she's like fifty percent with us and fifty percent someplace else. I think I've come to the conclusion that I like the old, chatty, excessively happy Lindsey a lot better than this emotional combo she's got going on now. Thinking about her emotions has me remembering back to all that I'd been going through and what Sasha and Krystal have already gone through. One time before, Krystal told me our powers were rooted to our emotions. I believe that now more than anything. And if that were so, looking at Lindsey now had me feeling all kinds of sorry for what she might be going through.

But what happens next keeps me from contemplating my fellow Mystyx's upcoming issues.

Twan reaches for the door, the one that will take us out of the back stairwell we were using and onto the first floor. We came this way because there were people everywhere in the library, trying to walk down the main steps was going to be like managing a mine field. There was no one in this back stairwell and we presumed that the door out would lead us right along the back sections of the first floor, where books on all types of mythology were stored.

But the door is locked.

Twan pulls at it a couple times, then turns to us. "Is an emergency exit supposed to be locked?"

Pushing Krystal and Lindsey behind me I move to stand right beside Twan. "No. I'm almost certain that would defeat the purpose."

I wrap my fingers around the knob and try to turn it, but it doesn't move. "Get back," I say.

I can hear the girls moving behind me. Twan only takes like a step back but he's still beside me.

Then someone else is there, too.

I can't see to my side because my flashlight is aimed in front of me and so are Twan's and the girls'. But pain strikes my arm and ricochets throughout my body. I fall sideways right into Twan, who readily catches me as my flashlight falls to the floor.

"Think you got the best of me, huh, tracker."

I hear the voice as I'm struggling to stand upright about a second before I take another blow to the stomach. Twan pushes me to the side then and I hear the connection of fist to flesh. I think Twan hit Mateo. I'm waiting for the adrenaline rush of power I've grown accustomed to feeling when struck or even just angered. But it doesn't come. Instead my *M* burns, and as I look over toward the girls theirs are glowing, too. As I stand up my fists clench at my sides and I push Twan out of the way before Mateo can strike him with whatever is in his hand.

Without even really seeing what Mateo has I lift a hand, catching his wrist before he can complete another swing. Something falls to the ground as I squeeze his wrist, but Mateo doesn't buckle and he doesn't wince in pain.

"Let's just go, man." I hear another voice and know it's Pace. "We're in enough trouble because of him."

"Shut up!" Mateo yells.

It's dark in the stairwell except for the flashlights still blaring and the colored light coming from our marks. Colored light that Pace and Mateo can now see but strangely haven't said anything about.

"I am not doing this," Pace says. "I'm through with this crap!"

Then Mateo does something I don't think any of us saw coming. He turns to Pace and opens his mouth, and from his mouth comes that yucky black smoke we're all used to seeing now. The smoke makes a beeline for Pace, hitting him right in the center of his chest, where it burns a black hole. Pace opens his mouth to scream but the sound dies. His eyes are black and lifeless as the dark smoke burns him from the inside out, until his lifeless body disintegrates into a pile of ashes on the floor.

As if summoned by the dark power being used, lights flicker on in the stairwell. It's a dim kind of light, like maybe the building's generator finally kicked in.

When Mateo turns again he's looking right at me, his head tilted eerily to the side, like his neck could actually be broken. He looks like Mateo but I don't think Mateo's in that body anymore. He smiles and then starts to chuckle. It's weird to see, but even stranger to feel the connection from him to me. It's dark and it's swirling and I feel the edges of the evil ripple along my skin. It's a familiar sensation, one I at one time believed was right for me. But now I know differently. I've chosen differently.

So with a nod of my head I send Mateo's body flying across the floor to slap into the door just under the neon-green Exit sign.

"What the hell is wrong with that dude?" Twan asks from behind me.

"Get the girls out of here," I tell him, sensing this fight isn't over.

"No doing," I hear Sasha say from behind. "We're not going anywhere."

"We're not leaving you, Jake," Krystal says.

"I told you before I've got your back, bro. So I'm not leaving either," Twan says.

I don't have a second to feel touched by their loyalty because demon-possessed Mateo is rising, coming straight at me with outstretched arms and smoke-spewing mouth.

The dark smoke touches my nostrils, moves upward slowly and I start to choke. It's familiar and sweet and intoxicating. But I'm stronger now. I've made a choice.

Lifting my open palm to Mateo I focus all my strength there, pushing him back to the wall, then twisting my hand so that he rolls over, away from me. He's writhing on the floor and I squeeze my fingers together, giving the effect of actually squeezing his neck. The darkness from his mouth swirls and forms shadows on the wall, two standing tall and seemingly looking down on Mateo's body. The shadows peel from the wall with spindly arms that reach for Mateo, pulling him out of my grasp. They cocoon him, I mean they literally wrap him in wave after wave of black smoke until he looks mummified.

"They'll take him back to Charon now," a voice from behind us states. Another voice I know.

I'm getting ready to turn to the voice when I hear a horrific cry and then Mateo's body, along with the shadows, are gone.

"Holy sh…man, what the hell?" Twan is saying. "This is wild. Did you see that?"

Sasha takes a step to him, putting a hand on his shoulder. "Yeah, I did. Sorry you had to, though."

"Nah, you kidding? That was like the coolest and scariest thing I've ever seen," he says.

"And you can never speak a word about it."

Oh, yeah, the man with the voice. Turning around, all of us look to the stairs where he's standing.

"Strickman," I whisper.

He starts to walk down the steps. "Yes, Jake. I told you

once before I knew what was going on, that I saw things the way they really were."

Sasha grabs my elbow, gasping. "He's not...ah...he's...um... not human," she finally manages to whisper.

"What?" I ask because really, I don't think I can take another shock today, or this month, or even this freakin' year.

"She's right," Strickman says. "I'm not human. And she can see me. That's interesting."

"Wait, what's going on now?" Twan asks.

"He." Sasha pauses to clear her throat. "He's got great abs," she manages finally.

Strickman smiles. Twan turns abruptly to Sasha. "What?"

"Ah, I mean, he's really built and has a nice chest and all if you don't count the fins or scales or whatever they are."

Tossing his head back, Strickman gives a full-bodied laugh.

"Instead of laughing at us don't you think you should explain?" I say.

"Really? He's got great abs?" Lindsey asks, still staring at Strickman, who to us is completely dressed in slacks and a shirt.

"I am from the Majestic," he says finally, coming to stand between us.

We're all surrounding him, staring like he's a new toy on Christmas morning. The girls are staring a little differently than me and Twan, but we're all interested in what he has to say.

"I'm the son of Pontus and Cylile."

When none of us respond, he continues, "My father was the god of the Deep Sea and my mother was a water nymph. Hence the gills, as we like to call them."

"Oh, my..." Lindsey gasps.

"Yes," Strickman says, smiling in her direction. "I am a god."

"Yep, he sure is," Sasha mumbles.

"A god? Here on Earth? In the Lincoln Library?" Twan asks, ignoring Sasha's remark. "You have got to be kidding me."

"Unfortunately, I'm not, and my presence here cannot be known. I trust you all understand that."

I'm already shaking my head. "No. I don't understand. What are you doing here? And when did Charon possess Pace and Mateo? Is that the reason they were bullying me all along?"

Strickman shakes his head. "No. That was strictly the boys and their inner issues."

"What were those shadows that took them?" Lindsey asks.

"Just that, Shadows. Everyone has them. They lie between the border of known and unknown. It's a form of a person's repressed self that can allow its mortal form to be possessed by a demon. That's how Charon takes over a mortal, he attacks their Shadow, bringing forth the rage and anger that has been festering there in the dark."

"Oh, my...excuse me," Lindsey says. "OMG, so my shadow can be possessed?"

Strickman shakes his head. "No. Not unless you have some festering rage or anger. Charon needs an evil energy source to feed from in order to possess."

"So whomever he possesses has to be inherently evil?" I ask. "Like me?"

"You were both, Jake. The Vortex that made a choice. And a good choice you made. I suspect Charon possessed these boys as a final warning to you. You're on opposite sides from him now, he's declared you his enemy."

"Gee, that just makes my day," I say with a sigh. "What else can go wrong?"

And just as I speak it, the building starts to shake.

"An earthquake?" Krystal asks.

"No. We're in the eye of the storm," Strickman says. "In the midst of Charon's clutches."

twenty-three

The rest of the night was long, with winds rattling the windows, children crying, grown-ups praying. There was a sort of silent chaos taking over the library.

We'd gone back up to the third floor, sitting in that back room with my dad, Twan's aunt, Krystal's parents and now Mrs. Hampton, Lindsey's legal guardian. It was weird, all of us, including Mr. Strickman, sitting around in one room, wrapped in blankets, silently anticipating the worst.

I wonder what they're all thinking. If anybody else is wondering if this is the end. A part of me doesn't really feel like it is. I feel sort of incomplete, like there's something left for us to do.

Strickman talks to our parents like they've known each other forever. Lindsey's guardian especially. I wonder if they know who and what he really is. And I wonder why he's really at Settleman's, since of course he didn't tell us.

I guess we're back to square one in the question-and-answer session. But you know what, I'm not all that mad about it now. I've learned a lot over the last few weeks, enough, I think, to last me for a good couple more weeks. What I don't know right now, I'm sure is coming. Just as I'm sure Charon's declaration is going to mean something big for me and the Mystyx.

"We'll all have to band together now." Krystal's mother speaks first. "We must protect them until their time comes."

Each of us—the Mystyx and Twan—all look back and forth at each other.

"Until what time comes?" Krystal asks her mother, who gives her a small smile.

"She means until it's time for you to battle with Charon again. The designated Guardians were put in place to prepare you for that time. Charon has gotten to most of them. Now, it's up to us, the mortal parents, to make sure you do what you were meant to do."

My dad says this and my mouth falls open.

Sasha's mother, who had kept her distance from us throughout the night, is silently crying, her hands covering her face as tiny sobs shake her body. I can see that Sasha's shocked that her mother has apparently known all along who and what she was. Her father's betrayal had seemed solitary but now, I think she's feeling it from them both.

Krystal doesn't look shocked that her parents know, which makes me believe she's had a clue as to their knowledge for some time now.

Even Twan's aunt doesn't look surprised. Lindsey's guardian looks as if this moment had been anticipated.

So had they all known? Was this an event in the making before we were even born? And what will happen now?

I don't know if it was morning or night, I just know that some more hours passed. We slept on the floors, woke up and ate the dried foods, drank the bottled water and sat around again, waiting for the storm to pass.

All the while more questions arise in my mind, but a state

of calmness keeps me from asking them. I wonder if that was Uncle William lending me a hand once again.

Or if it was just the calm before the big storm, not this warning we were apparently getting now. But the one that would forever decide our fate.

epilogue

The first night back in my bed and it feels heavenly. Not that I'm lying on a sleep-number mattress or anything plush like that, but it's my bed and it just feels good to be back in it. After three long days and two nights cooped up in the library with half the town of Lincoln, a cot on the porch with the open night air might have felt better.

So I'm back in my bed and tomorrow we're back in school. Next week is Thanksgiving. It's also the week of November twenty-first, when Barrow, Alaska, goes into its reported dark days. Sasha still thinks we'll end up there but me, the realistic one, says not. For one, my dad doesn't have money to send me to Alaska and he wouldn't even if he did. After winning the battle with Dumar and having me reinstated in school, his first goal is to see me graduated and accepted into a good college. He's still hoping I'll have some semblance of a normal life. Plus, what good would it be to go to Alaska? Charon can appear anywhere, he can strike here in Lincoln again just as he could across the oceans in China or something. It's not like he needs a passport or visa to travel.

Besides, Sasha saw more magicals in the library, saw their real faces beyond their earthly glamour. That proves there's something still lurking here in Lincoln, something we need to stay here to take care of.

My eyes feel all scratchy, so I close them to get some relief. Sleep comes quickly, exhaustion settling over me like a heavy blanket.

And then the dream begins...

I'm still in bed but I'm not alone. Krystal is there with me, lying right beside me, the hem of her nightshirt riding up so that my hand skims along the smooth skin of her thigh.

She makes this soft sound as we kiss, and every nerve in my body is on end. I'm tingling all over as our kiss deepens and I move so that I'm on top of her. One of my legs falls between hers, my palm moves up from her thigh to cup her unbound breast. And then she makes that sound again and I completely melt.

No, not melt. It's so hot, I'm sweating. My heart's beating wildly as I keep kissing her and she keeps kissing me. I don't know where we are except on a bed and I really don't care. I have no idea what's going on around me, only that her arms are wrapped tight around my neck, pulling me closer, urging me further.

"Krystal."

I hear her name, but it's not in my voice.

"Krystal."

There it is again, and I know I didn't say it because my lips are busily nipping a heated path down her neck.

"Yes," she answers, and at first I think she's just conceding to the pleasure I feel rippling through my body.

But no, she's not talking to me at all.

Pulling back, I'm alarmed to see there's nobody there. No Krystal, just me and my overexcited self. Turning around quickly I'm staring into darkness and a chilly breeze is now greeting my naked body. I reach somewhere, hoping to find some basketball shorts or something to cover myself. The last thing I want to do is get up from this bed and walk through endless darkness in the nude.

Like someone flicked on a switch, the pitch darkness turns blue, tinted slightly just as I remembered it before. I'm in the Underworld. Now I really want to find some shorts or pants. Fighting demons buff is so not going to work.

When I stand I already have shorts on, don't really know where they came from but I'm grateful just the same.

I hear her name being called again and she's answering.

"I hear you but I can't find you," Krystal says.

"I'm right here," I say. But again, I don't think she's talking to me.

I keep walking in the direction I hear the voices, both of them, the boy and the girl.

"Krystal, come on. I'm waiting," he says, and I swear the voice sounds familiar now.

"I'm coming," Krystal answers.

Something clenches in my chest at the sound of her voice. She's going to him. She knows who he is. She's always known.

After wandering down the longest hallway ever I see more blue light at the end and I hear the trickling of water. The River Styx.

Moving faster I try to get to the end before the ferry leaves, because I know instinctively there's a ferryboat docked in the water, with a hooded man and his staff waiting to pull off, to take another willing soul into the Underworld.

"Krystal," I call to her, hoping she'll hear me like she hears the other male voice. But she doesn't answer me.

"Krystal!" I yell louder and start to run.

Laughter answers me. Not demonic but evil just the same.

As I get to the end of the hallway and walk into the clearing I see the one laughing and my entire body freezes.

Franklin.

But then it's not him, at least not the way I remember seeing him when he was a student at Settleman's.

He's bigger now, his body like some teenage bodybuilder. He's wearing jeans and no shirt, his bronze chest glistening in the eerie blue light. His eyes are black but his mouth is smiling. And Krystal's walking straight toward him.

"Krystal, no," I shout, and she turns.

"I'm sorry, Jake. I have to go," she says, her hair a wild mess around her head, her eyes just a little wild as she glares back at me briefly.

"No! He's not who you think he is!"

"He's mine," she says, and the air escapes my lungs.

Falling to my knees I watch as she takes Franklin's hand and he lifts her onto the ferry. He's standing beside the robed man. Charon.

The laughter sounds again.

"No, Krystal," I say but my throat is hoarse from yelling for her. It's more like a croak and I know she can't hear me, but I tell her anyway. "You're mine. I'm yours."

Above the laughter the sound of rushing water roars, a wet breeze tickling my skin. "You're mine. I'm yours. Krystal, please."

And as I'm talking huge waves engulf me, carrying my body through what feels like the inside of a washing machine. I turn and twist and thump and fall. But all I can think about is her, all I can hear is the sound of her voice. All I can remember is the feel of her skin.

Krystal. Krystal.

My legs are kicking wildly, my arms flailing about. My heart feels like it's about to beat right out of my chest and then I sit right up in my bed. Sweat rolls down my face as I clench the sheets in both fists.

It was a dream. Just a dream, I'm trying to convince myself and catch my breath at the same time. Then my cell phone rings.

Krystal

He's got to be up. I know he is. He was right there, I felt him as if he were standing right next to me. The dream had been so intense. I could feel his kisses, his caresses. I wanted more and more. We were going all the way and I wasn't afraid like I thought I'd be.

When Franklin had first suggested sex to me I'd been deathly afraid. Maybe because it was with Franklin and I knew he wasn't the right person. But Jake, he was different. Everything about him was different.

Jake had as much emotional baggage as I did, which to me made us a great match because neither one of us were perfect. The fact that we both shared supernatural powers only solidified the fact that we should be together.

Or so I thought.

Until Franklin appeared in the dream.

All he'd had to do was call my name and I was following him, like a horse to a handful of carrots. And I don't think I really wanted to follow him, but there was something pulling me in that direction, telling me what to say, something very strong.

But Jake was there. He was coming for me. He said I was his and he was mine.

Jake was mine.

"Hello?" I hear his voice and almost scream with joy.

"Jake?"

"Krystal?"

"Did you see him? You were there, did you see him?"

"Did I see who? Where?" He doesn't sound like he was sleeping at all and I know that's because he's awake. He was in that dream with me and now he's awake.

"You were there, weren't you? In the dream with Franklin and…and—"

I can't say the name even though I can see the no-face demon clearly.

"And Charon."

With a sigh I fall back on my bed. "Yes."

Sasha

Tonight I'm looking for my moon, desperately needing the connection with another world, another time and place. Since learning I can astral project a feeling of solace has come over me. I know that I'm a human teenager, living on Earth and doing what a normal teenager's supposed to do. Then again, there's a more magical part of me that belongs in another world where I'm not considered strange but a kindred spirit.

Twan and I seem to be growing closer, and by that I mean he's hinting toward us getting more physical. I haven't told anyone, but I'm leaning in that direction myself. Something about the way I feel when he kisses me and touches me. My body tingles all over and at times I'm afraid I'll astral project or disappear. It's like I'm losing control of myself around him, though not in a bad way.

Last night he said he loved me. I believe every word because I love him, too. He knows who and what I am and he still loves me. I've never had that before and it feels good.

So sitting on the edge of my bed gazing out into the dark night sky I wish for my moon. And just like that the clouds seem to part and I see the giant orb clearly. I blink and then blink again because this doesn't look like my moon. It doesn't look altogether normal.

Standing, I move closer to the window and open it, leaning my face out until the chilly November breeze kisses my cheek. I study it a little closer.

It's not my normal moon because it's blue.

A blue moon on the first full moon of November. Flipping through my mental astronomy database I know that's not normal. Blue moons are the second full moon of each month. And this is early November. It's all wrong.

And yet…here it is.

A tiny sense of dread moves along my spine.

Lindsey

I've always heard voices, or thoughts I guess, from everyone else. Since I was younger I've heard their inner musings. After a while it became second nature and I figured out a way to handle it. Wear black and pray that at some point and time they did, too.

But that's not working now.

And I'm not just hearing their thoughts. I'm feeling their feelings and it's scaring the hell out of me.

I felt everything Jake was going through, the turmoil, the indecision, the pain.

And tonight, I felt more.

Panic and pain tore through my sleep so now I'm standing at the back door looking at the weirdest moon I've ever seen. The cool breeze is whipping around my body, making me intensely aware of the thin nightgown I'm wearing.

Looking up to the sky I'm wondering what's going to happen next, or more likely, how much more I can bear. If the thoughts of others weren't bad enough, the feelings will be enough to kill me. And I think that's his purpose.

Shivering, I wrap myself in my arms but I don't move. I don't run back into the house and climb under my covers. I stand right there, staring at that ghoulish moon, waiting for whatever it's bringing to come.

Waiting for my part in this battle to begin.

★ ★ ★ ★ ★

QUESTIONS FOR DISCUSSION

1. Have you ever been bullied? If so, how did it make you feel? Did you ever tell anyone? How was the situation resolved?

2. What do you think about kids who bully others?

3. Do you think, if Jake had said something sooner, Pace and Mateo would have stopped bullying him?

4. If you had Jake's power, would you have handled the bullying situation the same way?

5. Is it possible for people to be born evil, or do you think it's something they learn?

6. Should Jake have told Twan about the Mystyx powers? Or should he have tried harder to keep the secret?

7. Why do you think Jake really keeps thinking about Franklin?

8. Do you believe there are other life forms or supernatural powers?

9. Do you ever wonder about government conspiracies?

10. What if there was a real cover-up and there was another form of life, do you really want to know about it?

While writing this story I listened to lots of music, I do that a lot when I write. But this time I thought it would really give you some insight into Jake's struggles and triumphs if I shared that playlist with you. Hope you enjoy!

mayhem playlist

1. "Mine" by Taylor Swift

2. "Just the Way You Are" by Bruno Mars

3. "No Air" by Jordan Sparks and Chris Brown

4. "Dead and Gone" by TI featuring Justin Timberlake

5. "Over" by Drake

6. "If Today Was Your Last Day" by Nickelback

7. "Lose Yourself" by Eminem

8. "Diary" by Wale

9. "Not Afraid" by Eminem

10. "OMG" by Usher

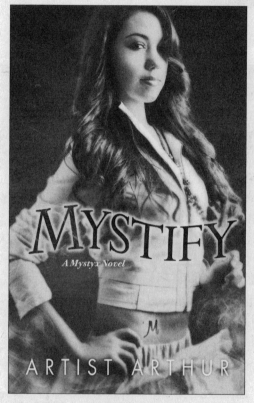

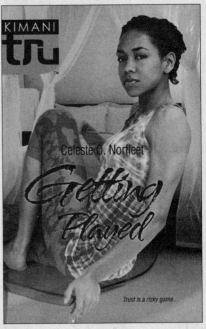

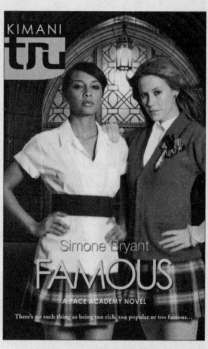

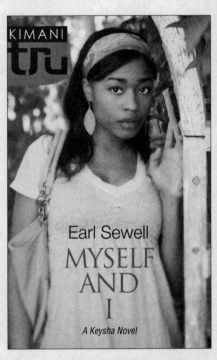